To Andy
My mate Spikey

HA

A SUMMER OF MASSACRE

Yours Sinfully

GARRY CHARLES

HADESGATE

PUBLICATIONS

Hadesgate Publications
PO Box 167
Selby
North Yorkshire
YO8 4WP

www.hadesgate.co.uk
www.hadesgateforums.co.uk
email: info@hadesgate.co.uk

Cover art and layout: Garry Charles
Additional art direction: Terry Cooper
www.terrycooper.co.uk

First published March 2007

ISBN 978-0-9550314-8-9

Prepared and printed by:
York Publishing Services Ltd
64 Hallfield Road
Layerthorpe
York
YO31 7ZQ
Tel: 01904 431213 Website: www.yps-publishing.co.uk

A BRIEF HISTORY OF HAMMERHEAD

It's funny how some projects come into being. It's a bit like planning to have a child, you haven't done it but all of a sudden your wife is pissing on a little stick and telling you she is up the duff. You're shocked, but pleasantly surprised at the same time. Bottle of pills or big, fuck off, cigar? You just don't know which way to turn. You're daunted by it all, but at the same time you know it's an important turning point in your life.

I've already done the child part twice, but I recently had a similar experience with the creation of the HAMMERHEAD novel. I had plans to write another novel because that's what writers do, but I had no intention of writing about a crazy fucker who lived in the woods and enjoyed the taste of human flesh. Like I said, it's funny how things come around when you least expect them.

At this point I'd forgive you for asking just what the fuck is this crazy fucker smoking? I can assure you it's nothing stronger than a menthol cigarette. All I want to do is explain a little about how HAMMERHEAD: THE NOVEL came into being.

It began just before Christmas 2006 when I picked up a copy of a relatively new magazine entitled 'GOREZONE'. I read the articles and decided to ring the editor, Bryn Hammond, and congratulate him on breaking into the mass market of newsagents and giving coverage to a genre that is sadly lacking and often sneered upon.

We got talking and Bryn told me all about a film he had directed a few years ago called THE SUMMER OF THE MASSACRE and how it was about to be reinvented with American funding and cast. He explained the ins and outs of the project and how they planned on commissioning a graphic book version. They would also be producing an action figure of the movie's villain, ED CRAVEN.

I wished him luck and he said his goodbyes before hanging up. I thought no more about it and moved on to working on a few short stories and a new novel. But two days later I received an email from the producers and they had an idea. They wanted someone to write a novel, but they didn't want anyone, they wanted me. I replied that I was very interested and so talks with Mark Bennett began.

He wasn't looking for a word for word, blow by blow novelisation. He wanted something slightly different. It was going to be my job to create an adaptation that would sit somewhere between the original movie and the new.

Under normal circumstances this would have been a piece of piss, but things are never that fucking easy. There were complications to be taken into consideration. All I would have to work on was a heavily censored version of the original movie and nothing else. The original screenplay was gone and lost forever. The new one was yet to be penned.

"No problem," I told them.

"Oh, fucking shit," I thought.

On the plus side I was given free reign to do whatever I wanted with the characters and their histories. I was told to write whatever I saw fit. With this in mind and the movie watched I set to work. The film was a throw back to classic horror and I wanted to do the same with the book. I wanted to give it a feel of early Shaun Hutson and Guy N Smith.

I started with Ed Craven and gave him a past, a reason for being and the producers immediately liked what I'd done and asked if they could add the scene at the start of the film. I continued to write and, within three weeks, the first draft was complete.

Both Mark and Bryn were pleased with the end result and started working other ideas into the screenplay as I moved onto the proofreading. With the help of C J Lines this was done in about a week and half. HAMMERHEAD had been born and he was one nasty little cunt. That version now sits in your hands and is waiting to be read.

I hope it makes your fucking toes curl and your stomach churn, but most of all I hope you enjoy it, you sick, twisted bastards.

I'll remove the duct tape and allow you to leave soon, but before we part ways, I must thank the following people who have helped make this novel possible.

Bryn Hammond, Mark Bennett, George and Anne Mcletchie. You guys started this thing and I'm glad to stand by your side until the bitter end. Thank you and here's to future projects.

C J Lines, your help, words of wisdom and friendship are much appreciated. I eagerly wait seeing your work in print.

To my wife and children; I'm sorry I make you suffer and thank you for forgiving me for writing on Christmas Day. I'm a bastard, but I love you all.

Ryan Nicholson, we have never met but I class him as a new friend and a fucking damn fine moviemaker.

Tim Sullivan, another maker of celluloid mayhem. I'm honoured to know you and I owe you one in the future.

Shaun Hutson, an inspiration and part-time mentor. I may not want to look like you did in the eighties anymore, but I follow in your footsteps nonetheless.

Finally – and most importantly – to you, the reader. You make us what we are and we only do it for you.

Garry Charles
Feb 2007

BLACKWOOD

BLACKWOOD 1983

The woods may have been encapsulated by the night, but that didn't mean they were sleeping. In fact the forest that surrounded Blackwood on three sides never slept. It was a place of dark menace and the townspeople knew it.

They would tell their children stories of the strange creatures that hid within the branches of the trees. Abnormal animals that waited patiently for young ones to wander off without their parents; waited until they could ensnare the young flesh and feed off it.

The children would lie in bed, the covers pulled up around their necks, and listen in fear as they learned about the grisly fate that awaited them, should they ever venture away from home. They would tremble as their gaze drifted to the bedroom window; a wooden frame that held a vision of the nightmare world that encroached on their very doorstep.

The adults, satisfied that their children had heeded the message would then kiss them on the cheek or the forehead, wish them good night and leave the room. Only then would they go around the house and check all the doors and windows, not once but twice. Every lock would be turned and then turned again as they gazed out into the winter's night sky and they would tremble with a fear of their own.

They knew that monsters in the true sense of the word didn't exist, yet they knew the forest held a deadly secret and they had no wish to find out if the rumours were true.

And then, with their homes secured tightly they would go to bed and sleep unsoundly, saying a prayer for the strangers that may inadvertently drive through the town once the street lights came on.

Oh, yes, it may have been dark in the woods but deep within the tightly knit woodland of trees and bramble, one house never slept.

Mother sat at the kitchen table and looked down at the food on her plate. She hadn't eaten in five days and she hungered to devour the meal laid out before her. Still she refused to touch it, even though the others had long since finished what she had prepared.

Father had gone upstairs to do whatever it was he did after the late dinner and she could hear the sounds of movement from the rooms above. He disgusted her, but she was his wife now and she had learned the hard way that she had to obey. Love and honour were unimportant in the relationship, but obedience was a statutory requirement for the role of Mother in the Craven household.

She looked across to her son in the corner and cringed at the sight of him playing happily.

"What is that, Simon?" she asked in a whisper.

"Edward gave it to me," the boy replied with a grin and held up the dead rat, its head a mangled mess of dried blood, brain matter and shattered bone.

Mother hated Edward as much as she hated Father and the thought of either of them touching her the way they did when they took her to the bedroom made her throat spasm. The smell of their unwashed skin against hers as they rubbed themselves against her brought tears to her eyes. But she would lay there and let them have their way. She had to obey. Rape was preferable to the punishment dealt out for disobedience and she had the scars to prove it.

"It's a toy," Simon added, pulling her away from the images of degradation that threatened to tear apart what remaining sanity she had.

"Well put it down," Mother scolded. "It's dirty."

"But, Mum. Edward gave it to me," Simon complained.
"Where is that boy?" She hadn't seen him since dinner.
Father had ordered her to ensure his son did not leave the house tonight and she would be beaten if she failed in her duties as stepmother to the boy that treated her no better than a whore.
"He went out to the shed to get me another toy," Simon replied, still tossing the dead rat from one hand to the other.
Oh, God. He's gone out. Mother could already feel the burn of leather strap whipping at her breasts for failing to comply with Father's words.
"Simon," she called. "Would you go and fetch Edward back indoors?"
"You told me to stay away from him," Simon replied awkwardly, a childlike response in retaliation for her earlier tone regarding the rat.
"Well now I'm telling you to go find him for me," she snapped unintentionally.
"Why don't you get him?" The boy had been around Father and Edward too long.
"You know I can't leave the house." Her voice trembled. "Please do this for your mummy," she pleaded.
"OK, don't have a fit." Simon saw the terror in his mother's eyes and he backed down, dropping the rat and getting up from the matted fur rug next to the open fire.
"Don't be long," his mother hissed. "It's dark out."
"I'll be two minutes," Simon promised with a shake of his head, leaving via the back door and leaving Mother sat at the kitchen table.

He walked along the rear porch. He felt sorry for Mother, but he was only eight and what more could he do to help? He already did all the chores that Father gave him and he did extra when Edward told him to. And Edward wasn't that bad all of the time. Yes, he was mean, rude and quite often he would unleash torrents of violent physical and mental abuse upon Simon's tiny frame, but sometimes he was almost nice. After all he had given Simon the toy to play with.

Things could be worse.

But they could also be better if Mother just went along with the new way of life. At the very least he would have liked to see her eat. He knew the meat wasn't chicken, but it tasted like it and was filling. She really should eat to keep her energy up.

Simon pushed thoughts of Mother away as he stepped down from the porch and into the back yard. The ground had already been coated in a fine layer of frost and it stabbed through his socks and into the palms of his feet. He looked across at the shed, the single bulb from within casting only a dim light into the surrounding forest, but still enough for Simon to see by.

He ran, his feet quickly turning numb as the pain of coldness travelled up to his ankles. He wished they'd not taken his shoes. He wouldn't have run away. He couldn't have done that. He couldn't leave Mother alone here.

He reached the shed and pushed on the door, causing it to swing open and bang loudly against the workbench just inside.

"Edward?" Simon called. "Mother wants you back in house."

"Yes, in a minute," Edward's voice replied. "But first I want to show you something." The request was followed by a quick succession of hammering noises.

Mother fidgeted in her chair. Simon had been gone longer than she expected and she was worrying. She didn't like his being with Edward. The boy was older than Simon by quite a few years and the thought of them alone together filled her with dread. If she could have gone for him she would have, but she wasn't permitted to leave the house.

A woman's place is in the kitchen or the bedroom. Father's words echoed in her memory.

Her stomach rumbled before cramping painfully and she looked down at the dinner plate with longing. She didn't want to eat. She wanted to starve, wanted to waste away and die. At least then it would be over for her. But what of Simon? What would happen to her darling boy if she was gone?

She fought the sickness in her stomach and raised the fork from the table. She still wouldn't touch the foul meat they forced her to cook, but she would make herself eat the vegetables that sat cold on the chipped china. She would just have to ignore the juice that ran from the undercooked flesh and covered the base of the plate with its liquid redness.

Slowly she raised the potato to her mouth and bit down on it, her stomach rebelling against her need to feed. She chewed and swallowed, but it didn't stay down.

She was still retching up acidic bile when the back door was pulled open. She felt the chill breeze from outside stroke the sweat on her forehead, but she couldn't look up, her body bent rigid as a final bout of dry heaving tore at her throat.

Finally she managed to speak. "Did you find him, Simon?"

"Yes." The reply didn't come from her little boy. "He found me."

EDWARD!

Mother turned cold at the harshness of her stepson's voice, not daring to look up from the small circle of vomited potato, stomach lining and hint of blood.

"We played a game," Edward continued. "But I got bored."

"Simon?" Mother cried.

Simon didn't reply to her call, but Edward laughed softly.

"He can't hear you." From his place at the door Edward tossed something small and pink.

It landed in the pool of sick between Mother's feet with a small, wet splash. For a moment she tried to figure out what the object was and then quickly wished she hadn't. At the realisation of what had hit her, she felt the scream rise from deep within herself.

"What did you do to my baby?" Mother screamed as she tore her stare away from the severed ear.

"We played a game." Edward grinned as she looked up, tapping the clawed end of the hammer against his blood stained jeans. "He lost."

"You bastard!" Mother jumped upright and lunged, but the chain at her ankle only allowed for limited movement, the metal jarring her leg and sending a rod of agony up to the base of her spine.

Edward giggled as he approached her, feeling in his shirt pocket before fishing out two sticky orbs that he dropped casually on to Mother's plate.

"He has your eyes," Edward teased as he raised the hammer.

"BASTARD!" Mother screamed in anger, lashing out savagely at her son's murderer.

Her nails dug into Edward's cheek and tore four trenches of flowing crimson from just below his left eye down to his upper lip. He paused, the hammer held above his head as he grinned at Mother.

"Bitch." He brought the hammer down with vengeful speed.

Mother didn't have time to back away, the hammer head shattering her skull on impact and powering down into her brain. Bright lights danced before her eyes for only the briefest of moments and then the life drained from her face.

Edward held her upright, pulling her closer. And then, very tenderly he kissed her on the lips.

"Goodnight Mother." Pulling the hammer free he let her fall in a heap at his feet.

"What the fuck is going on down here?" Father barrelled in to the kitchen and froze.

"Hello, Father," Edward grinned.

"Not again," Father sighed. "She was a bloody good cook." He turned on Edward and smashed a fist into his son's face.

Edward fell to the floor as blood poured from his broken nose, the hammer skidding across the floor and coming to rest near the fireplace.

"Do you know how hard it is to find a new family?" Father hollered. "I'm going to teach to you a lesson you'll never forget." He kicked out at Edward as he made his way to the sink.

"I'm sorry," Edward blubbered from his place on the floor.

"You will be," Father promised.

Father sank his hand into the filthy wash water and found the handle of the paring knife. As he wiped the blade on his trousers he marched back towards his son.

"Father," Edward whimpered.

"Shut up and take it like a man," Father yelled in Edward's face, pinning the boy to the floor with his knee. "This is gonna hurt."

Edward tried in vain to fight, but Father was bigger and stronger. He forced his son's mouth open with one hand, prying the jaw as wide as it would go. He worked quickly with the knife, utilising years of skilled butchery as he severed the tongue and pulled it clear of Edward's teeth. He held the limp muscle up above Edward and let it bleed down on his son.

"You won't be back talking now." As he stood up he threw the tongue across the room. "Get this fucking mess cleaned up."

Edward tasted his own blood, hot and coppery as it ran down the back of his throat. The pain in his face was overshadowed by the fire of hatred that now burned in his belly. He waited until Father turned away and then he struck.

He dived across the Kitchen and snatched up the hammer in both hands, swinging himself around and rushing towards Father.

The first blow glanced off the side of the old man's head, but it was still enough to send him staggering along the hallway. Before Father could regain his composure, Edward hit him again. This time the claw smashed through skull and pierced the mushy cerebellum. Using the claw like a hook Edward dragged him back to the Kitchen, only pulling the hammer free when he had the old wretch laid out on the table.

He rolled Father onto his back. He wanted to look in his eyes before he finished the job. He may not have been able to answer back, but Father would get Edward's point.

The hammer came down again and again, pulverising the face until it was nothing more than a red smear that stained the old wood of the table top. Even then, Edward kept swinging, beating down until he collapsed from exhaustion.

He didn't need Father. He'd collect his own family.

THE SUMMER

ONE

Curt Hutson stood and, shielding his eyes, looked up at the imposing structure that was Daventry University. He wasn't usually the type to be interested in architecture and all that shit, but for some reason he felt he must take it all in.

Over the last three months he'd seen it everyday without fail but now, as he prepared to leave for the summer, it didn't look as familiar. The large windows stared back at him, row upon row of oversized rectangle eyes held within the vicious grip of weathered brick and eroded limestone. The roof took on the appearance of a wide brimmed hat that had been pulled down to hide the features of an unknown face. For the first time since signing up, Curt found the place unnerving. It sent a shiver down his spine.

"Fuck you," he whispered at the building. "See you in seven weeks, arsehole." He lowered the hand from his eyes and gave Daventry the finger.

He turned back to the van and, in an attempt to shake the uneasiness that had crept into his gut, he decide to recheck his packing. Anything was better than having to face the University again. The others would be here shortly and then it would be party time.

Well, almost party time. The detour to Katie's parents would have to be made first. She had some important news to give them before they could head out to the coast.

"Seven weeks of sea, sand and drinking 'til we puke," Curt said to no one in particular as he yanked open the sliding door of the van with a squeak that set his teeth on edge.

He couldn't wait for them to get away from it all; the stresses of degree courses and six thousand word essays were starting to grind on his good nature, and the time to just be old reliable fun loving Curt would do him the world of good. Shit, they all needed to wind down. It had been a hard year and they deserved some relaxation and fun.

As Curt slowly sorted through the cases and boxes of beer, a smile crept across his face at the thought of his friends' reactions when they saw his parents' beach house. Not that it was really a beach house; it was more a static caravan, but over the years his mum and dad had worked wonders with it. They'd taken the time and effort to add all the little touches that made it a home from home. Dad had built the front porch and the window boxes. He'd also laid out an intricate patio with brick barbeque. He'd made a wonderful job of it all and Curt was sure his friends would love it. Then there was the view; nothing but sea until it met the horizon. You stepped out of a morning to find yourself within spitting distance of the beach. It was an amazing place and it would easily erase any bad memories of the past year and its non-stop, boring lectures.

Whilst Curt made a third attempt at rearranging space in the car, a taxi pulled in from the main road and pulled up next to the van. The rear doors opened and the quiet morning was definitely over.

"Where on earth did you find this piece of shit?" Judy Barker howled hysterically as she ran from the taxi and circled the pale blue van.

"This, my dear lady, is no piece of shit," Curt replied, sticking his grinning face out of the door. "This is the Hutson Shag Wagon." He flicked his tongue out at her and she laughed harder.

"No, no, it's a piece of shit," Judy teased.

"Where's Katie?" Curt asked as he looked around for his other friend.

"Oh damn." Judy quickly turned serious. "I left her to unpack the taxi."

Curt jumped from the van and rushed around to the other side, grabbing Judy's hand and dragging her along.

"How could you do such a thing?" Curt joked. "And with Katie in her delicate situation." Curt chuckled as they rounded the back of the van.

"There you are," Katie Frost scowled at them as they came into view. "Would one of you be kind enough to pay the driver?"

"Cheeky cow," Curt said, already pulling his wallet from his back pocket.

"But what about my delicate position?" Katie threw back at him without a pause.

"You're pregnant, not skint." Curt elbowed her playfully as he brushed passed her.

"Watch the baby," Katie punched his shoulder and giggled.

Curt feigned injury, rolling his arm and flinching as he leaned down to face the driver.

"How much, mate?"

"Sixteen quid." The driver held out a hand.

Curt withdrew a twenty and handed it over. "Thanks and keep the change."

"Cheers," the driver said, already rolling the window up and restarting the car.

Curt and Judy took the bags. They may have joked about Katie's pregnancy but they realised it was a touchy subject. She'd kept it a secret until it had started to show, the only hints being that she'd told everyone she was quitting the drink and that smoking was off the list of things she'd be doing. They'd taken it as a health fad and ribbed her about it until she'd told them why.

But that was all she'd told them. She still refused to talk about the father, only saying that he wasn't interested in having a kid and she was fine with that. They didn't push her on it. They were close friends and she would tell them when she was good and ready. Maybe after she'd spoken to her parents she would confide in them the secret of the dad to be. If not, it didn't matter. No matter what happened they'd be there for her when the time came. They were more than just friends, they were almost a family.

"Hey, you guys." The sound of Josh Lebbon's voice echoed from across the car park. "Don't go leaving without me," he shouted as he came into view.

"Get a fucking move on," Katie yelled back. "We're ready to go."

"Don't lie to me," Josh replied. "You haven't even finished packing that piece of shit."

"It's not a piece of shit," Judy laughed. "It's the Hutson Shag Wagon." Before the sentence was finished she was doubled over again and tears were running down her face.

"Looks more liked the shagged wagon to me." Josh eyed up their mode of transport and shook his head. "Where the hell did you find this rust bucket?"

"Don't insult Christine, she doesn't like it." Curt lovingly stroked the side of the van.

"Man, you gotta stop it with the horror films," Josh warned as he tossed his bag into the back of the Shagged Wagon.

"You should have been around our flat last night," Judy managed to say between giggling. "We had a night long marathon of movies and Katie nearly shit herself."

"Nice mental picture going on here." Josh wrinkled his nose up.

"I did not shit myself," Katie defended herself. "The only problem I have at the moment is needing to piss all the time."

"Mental image is now damaging my brain," Josh growled as he fell to his knees in mock agony, hands clasped to the sides of his head.

"Get up, you idiot." Katie kicked his thigh.

The sound of an approaching car brought a stop to the joking. Josh got back on his feet and they all turned to watch, as the BMW crept towards them and pulled to a stop alongside the van. The black car came to a smooth stop and the window whirred downwards on electric motors to reveal the friendly face of Professor Reilly – Head of the History Department.

"Looks like you guys are ready to have some fun," the Professor remarked with his usual soft tone.

"Seven weeks of freedom," Judy sang. "No more lectures."

"I thought you enjoyed my talks on the New England settlers." Reilly looked genuinely hurt.

"It's not that," Judy stammered, embarrassed. "It's just…" She went blank.

"I know." Reilly smiled. "It's the holidays." The gentle smile returned to his face. "Just drive safely and have fun."

"You too, Professor," Judy said with a tiny wave.

"See you in seven weeks." Reilly returned the wave and drove off, the window rolling up as he pulled out into the main street.

"*You too, Professor,*" Curt mimicked Judy's farewell. "*I want to hug you and kiss you.*" He danced around her as he continued.

"Fuck you," Judy replied with a smile of embarrassment. "He is sexy though." She hid her face in her hands.

"He's a fucking arsehole," Katie whispered under her breath and climbed in the van. "Let's get going." She flopped down onto one of the makeshift seats in the back.

"What's up with you?" Josh asked. "Mood swings?"

"Piss off," Katie quickly lost any good feelings about the first day of the holidays and fell into a quiet sulk.

"Just leave her be," Curt said as he climbed in behind the steering wheel. "You know telling her parents is going to tough on her."

"Sorry," Josh sat opposite Katie. "I'm sorry, Katie."

"Just forget about it, Lebbon." Katie turned away from him and gazed absentmindedly through the rear window.

"OK, folks. If we're all ready let's hit the road," Curt announced and turned the key in the ignition.

The engine grumbled once and then farted.

"Told you it was a piece of shit," Judy complained.

"Don't diss the Shag Wagon," Curt warned without any seriousness and tried the ignition for a second time.

The engine groaned as it attempted to turn over and then, with a bang and a roar it came to life, shaking the dashboard as it over-revved.

“It’s alive,” Josh yelled in his best Frankenstein voice.

With a mixture of moods fighting within the confines of the van, they set off for the start of the holidays.

BLACKWOOD 1997

"But you said we'd stop at a hotel," Ricky King bleated, refusing to leave the passenger seat of the parked car.

"I know what I said, but this'll be fun," David Herbert did his best to placate her. "I promise."

"And I know what your promises mean," she carried on in the whiney voice that made him want to throttle her.

"Have it your way," he snapped and backed off.

Why do I put up with her? He eyed Ricky up from a safe distance. His gaze moved down from her face to her low cut top. *That's why.* He watched her tits jiggle as she shifted in the seat. *That and the fact that she fucks like a minx.* With this in mind he left her to it, knowing without doubt that she'd come around.

He walked around to the rear of the car and opened the boot so he could unload the camping gear he'd stuffed in there late last night. Late enough so that his wife, Suzy, was sound asleep and wouldn't catch him in the act. She thought he was on an all expenses paid weekend business trip. It would have looked extremely bad if she'd seen him furtively filling the car with a tent and supplies.

The idea of what she'd do if she found out about Ricky filled him with dread. After all, the office junior sat in his Ford Escort was nothing more than sex. It would be devastating if he lost everything over a piece of fluff. Not that a divorce from Suzy would be a bad thing, she annoyed him more than Ricky, but the thought of losing the house and half of the savings he'd spent so long accumulating made him feel sick. Oh, no, the divorce would happen, but when it did it would be on his terms and not hers. He'd rather kill the frigid cunt than let her walk away with what was rightfully his.

He looked up from the bags and stared at the back of Ricky's head, the short hair revealing her slender neck and smooth shoulders. He glanced up into the rear view mirror and saw her looking back at him through narrowed eyes.

Ricky saw him in the mirror and scowled at him.

Bastard. She kept the insult to herself, making only an audible *humpf* noise as she fold her arms under her breasts. *How dare he bring me out here? I deserve better than this shit.*

Or did she? She was, when all was said and done, only his mistress and what did that entitle her to?

More than trip to the middle of shitsville forest.

She glanced over her shoulder and watched as David moved the back packs away from the car and her anger was quickly tinged with a mild arousal as he bent over, his already tight trousers pulling taut over his well formed buttocks. She shook her head, pushing away the carnal thoughts of his naked body pressing down upon hers.

He's not getting it that easily.

David laid the packs against the base of what he thought was a sturdy oak, though in all truth he didn't know if it was really an oak. He knew nothing about wild flora or fauna and didn't care either. All he was interested in was getting Ricky out of the damn car.

He grinned. *Time to play my joker.*

From the side pocket of one of the packs he took a tiny black box and held it in the palm of his hand.

'If this doesn't bring you around then I'm fucked.'

He watches them from the bushes with the intensity of an animal hunting its prey. He is eager to strike but he wants to savour the moment for as long as he can.

He sniffs the air, picking up the scent of the female's excitement. He knows little about the true nature of sex, but he has smelt this aroma on more than one woman and he knows where it will lead. He likes this smell, the heady musk of the moist area nestled high up between her legs. The area on Mother he was allowed to taste from as Father watched. It rouses feelings that confuse him, yet spur on his need to strike.

He grunts quietly in anticipation of the moment when her scent will be replaced by that of terror and hot urine. That is the moment he likes best, that special time when they realise that he is the master and that they are lost.

"David," Ricky cried with joy. "It's beautiful." She held the box as she appraised the ring in its velvet centre.

"Nothing's too beautiful for you," David added, "and, if you want, we can still go to a hotel."

"I love you," she whispered before throwing her arms around his neck.

"I know, babe." He nuzzled her.

"And the hotel isn't important as long as we're together," she said in his ear.

Gotcha, he thought happily.

After long moments of hugging and pledges of undying love from Ricky, which David returned with far less honesty, they finally pulled away from each other.

David had noticed that Ricky had been crying against his shoulder, but he didn't mention it. Everything was back on track and the weekend could really get started.

"We'd better get moving," he said as he helped Ricky out of the car, slamming the door and locking it behind them

"Where are we?" Ricky asked as she stood up straight, stretching her back and revealing a band of toned stomach.

"It's called Blackwood," David explained. "I wanted somewhere quiet and out of the way so we didn't have to worry about anything or anybody else."

"It's lovely," she sang as she spun around on her heels, the sun breaking through the tightly meshed ceiling of green and dancing across her moving frame.

"I just wanted it to be me and you." David smiled the smile of a well practiced cheat.

"It's perfect," Ricky stated, any lingering ideas of hotels and room service swept away and forgotten about.

"Like I said, babe," David flashed his teeth, "anything for you."

Ricky came to a stop and wavered on the spot until the dizziness left her. Only then did she attempt to walk past David.

"Come on then." She grabbed the smaller of the two packs and threw it on with ease. "Let's find a nice spot and then you can get your hands on these." She lifted her top and flashed the firm breasts held tightly in place with a white, lacy bra.

"Good idea." David rushed up beside her and struggled with the larger pack before lifting the tent bag under his arm. "No time like the present."

Ricky took David's free hand and, with patches of sunlight warming their faces, they entered the bramble lined pathway into Blackwood.

He watches as he fondles the hammer, running his fingers over the rusted, blood stained head with the attention of a long time lover. This hammer has served him well. So have many others over the years, but this one is his favourite. It's been with him ever since Father died and it's like a little brother to him. Whenever he goes hunting he takes it with him, a good luck charm of sorts.

He follows them stealthily until he's sure where they are heading and then he moves away, increasing his speed despite the limp that would hamper another's progress. As he winds his way between the trees and the undergrowth he keeps a close eye on his prey. He will soon be in front of them and he can still smell them on the breeze, but a good hunter never loses sight of the target. Father taught him that a long time ago.

His breath becomes deep and heavy, interspersed with panted yelps and guttural attempts at what could be words. He swings the hammer, drumming a beat against his thigh in rhythm with his breathing.

The hunt is almost over and he can feel the pounding of his heart as the moment of the kill looms ever closer.

The clearing was only small, but David could tell that Ricky loved it and he had to agree with her choice of location. The treetops had opened out and they now allowed the sun free access, warming the air around them and the woodland ground beneath their feet. It also added a new dimension to the foliage, giving everything a fresh vibrancy. It was as if the solar rays had awoken shades of green that had never been seen by human eyes.

"Right then," David said as the tossed the tent and the pack to one side. "Let's sort the accommodation."

"I'll help." Ricky dropped to her knees at his side, opening the tent bag and pulling out a handful of structure poles.

"Haven't you forgotten something?" David asked, raising a hand to her right breast and rubbing the nipple beneath the soft fabric of her top.

"You're an animal," she giggled, pushing forward to increase the pressure of his touch.

He can smell her musk so strongly now that he jumps from foot to foot like a giddy child, the blood pounding in the ragged remains of his ears, through his veins, with the heat of the hunt.

He raises the hammer to his masked face and kisses along the length of the shaft. He gurgles sloppily as the woman lays back and the man follows her down. The excitement is too much. He leaps from his place amongst the trees and charges at them.

Ricky moaned with pleasure as David's tongue forced its way into her mouth. She drove her own against his, tasting stale tobacco as she ran it across his teeth.

As they kissed she pulled at the zip on his jacket and then set to work on the row of buttons that lined the front of his shirt. She gained entrance and thrust her hand inside, running her fingers through the thick, coarse hair that covered his chest.

David followed her lead, yanking up her top and pushing the bra over the twin mounds of her tits. Without hesitation his fingers went to work on her nipples, twisting the fleshy lumps between finger and thumb.

Ricky arched her back at his touch. He was rough, but it turned her on more than he knew. She felt the hot flush of arousal between her legs and groaned deep in her throat. Still locked at the lips, she pulled him backwards.

David moved with her, showing eager willingness. He was already hard and wanted nothing else but to feel himself inside her. As David nuzzled the end of his penis between Ricky's warm thighs he saw only the briefest hint of movement from the corner of his eye. An instant later the side of his head erupted in blinding agony.

Ricky opened her eyes as David's lips were torn away from hers, and saw the side of his head suddenly change shape. The left eye bulged between the upper and lower lid and then exploded from the socket, stretching the optic nerve, before falling against his cheek.

David mumbled gibberish as he slowly stood upright, swaying unsteadily as pain ravaged his confused mind.

"What's wrong?" Ricky sobbed, unable to look away from the odd profile that, only moments before, had been David's face.

He whoops as the hammer collides with the prey's head, thrilled at the feel of warm blood as it sprays up the back of his hand.

He doesn't stay to watch as the stunned cattle staggers aimlessly around. He follows the swing of the hammer, running back into the forest and out of sight. Only once hidden does he turn to admire the injury he has dealt. He grunts in satisfaction as the female looks at her mate in shock and he is treated to that first smell of bitter urine.

He screams out as he decides to go in for the kill, leaping from his hiding place and clearing the short distance between himself and the cattle in no time at all.

He hollers out a death cry and leaps into the air and, as he comes down, he swings the hammer.

The top of his cattle's skull falls apart and it collapses as nothing more than fresh meat for the cellar.

Ricky finally screamed as the figure landed astride her and brought the unseen weapon down on David's head. She heard the skull break and, through tears, witnessed what was left of her lover's face fall in on itself, his body crumpling to the moss lined ground.

For what felt like an eternity she was frozen in place, unwilling to communicate as shock took a hold of her system. She couldn't move as the killer bent down and examined his kill, reaching out with a free hand and plucking the eyeball free from the decimated face.

She looked up as he turned to face her, pushing the eyeball through a gap in his expressionless mask. Ricky felt vomit rise as he clamped it between his teeth and began to chew. The first bite resulted in a wet *pop*. As he fed, opaque drool ran down the chin of the flesh-like mask.

Ricky suddenly moved, her foot kicking out at the killers groin and making satisfactory contact. He bent over, dropping the hammer at his feet and cupping his midsection as he howled like nothing human. Survival became Ricky's foremost thought and she moved with a speed that surprised her. She grabbed the hammer, gagging at the feel of the blood that still slicked the handle. With a scream she swung the hammer sideways at the monster. The aim was bad, the steel head bouncing off the killer's shoulder. To her relief, it was still enough to knock him off his feet.

She scanned the clearing, searching for the way they'd entered. The monster moaned behind her and she made her choice, running towards the pathway she could only hope would take her back to the car.

"Oh fuck, oh fuck," she muttered under her breath as she ran. "Oh fuck, oh fuck."

She ignored the thorny brambles as they tore at her bare arms and stomach, the pain outshadowed by the fear of death. If she could make it to the car she would be safe. All she had to do was keep running and not look back. As soon as she thought this, she slowed to look over her shoulder and saw him. She tried to scream, but all that came out was a hoarse warble, her throat

dry and sore.
"Oh fuck." She ran.

He hurts.

They have never fought back before and he blames himself. He was rash in the attack, acting on pure animal instinct alone. The human part that lived at the back of his mind had been swallowed by a primal desire to kill, to feed.

Now he is paying the price and the woman has escaped. He follows her, but she is fast and he is in pain.

Then he remembers the car and he knows where she is heading. The prey is always predictable and that is why they are so easy to hunt. He will have her soon and she will pay for what she has done to him.

He can see her up ahead and, as he cuts into the forest, she turns. For only a moment, their eyes lock. He chuckles at her feeble attempt of calling for help and the fire of the hunt returns, fuelled on her fear.

Ricky's lungs burned and her legs threatened to give out. She needed to stop, but knew that she couldn't do that. She glanced over her shoulder and took hope from the fact that she'd lost her pursuer. Maybe she would make it after all. She saw the car and those hopes were boosted further.

She forced her legs to pump harder as the vehicle drew closer, but then she stopped.

"Keys," she cried.

She slowed her pace, hoping beyond hope that David had left them with the car.

He waits until she arrives and he's happy to see that the fight is gone from her. She is ready for the taking. He doesn't move until she reaches the car. He's playing with her now. He's having fun.

Ricky approached the car, sobbing gently as she realised the keys wouldn't be left in the car. David loved his car more than anything and he'd never leave it unlocked.

She leaned against the side and dropped down slowly, curling her knees up and hugging them to her body. She closed her eyes and she cried.

He moves slowly and silently, taking pleasure in the sound of her sadness and the smell of terror ridden sweat that coats her from head to toe. He stands above her and looks down, reaching out a hand and stroking her hair.

Ricky felt the touch and lifted her head with a start. The last thing she saw was the hammer speeding towards her face.

TWO

"Pull over," yelped Josh as yet another bout of travel sickness turned his guts upside down.

"Quick," Katie added a plea of her own as the threat of being covered in Josh's breakfast reared its ugly head.

"Shit," swore Curt as he swung the dull steering to one side and unceremoniously left the road.

Josh was playing with the handle and had the side door rolling open before the van had even come to a stop; it was still coasting as he leaped for the outside world and the freedom to empty his gut.

"Wurgh!" He gripped his stomach and bent at the waist as pale green fluid spewed from his mouth and nose, most of which went over the rear wheel of the van.

"That's disgusting." Katie had seen enough of her own vomit every morning recently and she didn't need to see anyone else's.

"Sor…" Josh started to say. "Wurgh!" He was cut off as his stomach heaved and dislodged what felt like his entire intestinal tract.

"Why didn't you take something before we left?" asked Judy, her grinning face bobbing out of the open passenger window.

"I'm not usually this bad in a car." Josh wiped bile from his chin with the back of his hand. "I didn't realise we'd be travelling in the shake shack." He transferred the residue from his hand to the backside of his jeans.

"I've warned you about saying bad things about the van, mate," Curt said.

"Fuck you," Josh snorted and spat before climbing back into the van.

"You stink," Katie complained, wrinkling her nose in distaste. "What did you have for breakfast?" She held a hand over her face in a feeble effort to ward off the acidic stench.

"I finished off the fish and chips from last night," Josh answered, shrugging his shoulders. "They must have been off."

Whilst Josh had been throwing up the leftover supper, Curt had been rolling a joint, which he now lit up and took a deep drag from.

"What are you doing?" Judy snapped. "No smoking, remember." She nodded in Katie's direction. "Pregnant lady on board."

"I don't know about the lady part, but I'll give you the pregnant bit," Curt joked. "Anyway, I need a piss." He took the joint and left the van, heading in the direction of the bushes.

"Are you going to be OK from here on?" Judy asked with genuine concern, as she looked at Josh's pale face.

"I don't think there's anything left to bring up," he replied. "If it happens again I'll throw up my own arsehole." Despite feeling lousy, he managed a smile.

"Now you come to mention it, where are we?" Katie asked.

"I'm not sure," Judy said. "You fell asleep and Curt said he knew a shortcut."

"Yeah, he found Blackwood on the map," chipped in Josh.

"Blackwood?" Katie frowned.

"That is where your parents are from?" Judy already had a sinking feeling in her gut that she knew the answer.

"No," Katie stated irritably. "I've never heard of the place."

Judy swung back around in her seat and shouted out of the window. "Curt, you stupid arse."

"What?" came his disembodied reply, followed by a plume of thick smoke.

"You've gone and got us lost," she yelled back.

"No I ain't." Curt came back into view, fiddling with his fly as he walked. "Blackwood's about twenty minutes that way." He pointed straight ahead.

"That'd be great if we were going to Blackwood." Judy was doing her best to remain serious, but the look of confusion on Curt's face was comical.

"What?" he asked and she had to laugh.

"What?" His anger flared and he stormed towards the van. "What?" He leaned in through the side door and addressed Katie. "You said your folks came from Blackwood."

"No," Katie snapped. "I said they came from Blackmoore."

Josh, still recovering from gut ache joined Judy in laughing as Curt sputtered at Katie.

"What's so fucking funny?" shouted Curt which only sent the other two into further fits of hysterics.

"Your face is a picture," chuckled Judy.

Curt pulled the door shut on them, thumping it with the side of his fist and then marching around the back of the van. As he got to the roadside he took a cursory glance up and down the country lane and saw nothing, no other travellers on the back road at all. The idea that he had really got them lost left him feeling unsettled and did nothing to improve on the bad mood that was quickly winding its dark fingers around his consciousness. He walked along the side of the van and listened to his friends laughing at him.

"I should make one of you bastards drive," he yelled, causing the sound of mirth to increase.

"Just give me the map," he ordered as he pulled the driver's door open.

"Calm down," laughed Josh. "Smoke another joint."

"I'll smoke you if you don't give me the fucking map," Curt threatened.

Unable to stop laughing, Josh picked up the crumpled map and threw it over the top of the headrest.

"Now, let's see." Curt spread the map out on the seat and scanned the coloured pattern of intersecting roads. "Katie, where are we going?"

"Blackmoore." She stopped giggling long enough to answer.

"OK, people. Things aren't as bad as they look." Curt traced a finger over the map. "But we'll have to go to Blackwood first and fill up the Shag Wagon or we'll end up stuck out here."

"Can't we just head back to the main road?" queried Katie.

"Look, it's only a short detour and then we'll be back on the main road," insisted Curt. "I know what I'm doing."

"A detour!" Josh wailed in an over the top manner. "Haven't you seen The Hills Have Eyes?" Once again he cracked up.

"That's America, you dumb twat," replied Curt, climbing back into the van and starting it up. "That kind of thing never happens here." He fired up the engine on the first attempt and pulled back out onto the road.

"I wish this thing had a radio," complained Judy after another hour of driving. "This is getting dull."

"Then read a magazine," suggested Curt.

"Or fall asleep like Josh here," added Katie.

"I'm not tired and I don't read unless I really have too," Judy replied.

"Don't or can't?" asked Curt mischievously.

"Wanker." Judy swivelled in her seat to face the rear. "Hey Katie, what are you going to tell your parents?" she asked.

"Not much." Katie remained unforthcoming on the subject of the baby.

"But you're going to tell them who the father is?" Judy fished for the hundredth time.

"All I'm gonna tell them is that I'm having the baby," responded Katie. "The father doesn't come into it."

"But..."

"But, nothing," Katie interrupted. "He's made it clear he's not interested and that's the end of it." To signal an end to the conversation, Katie rolled over and closed her eyes.

Josh's idea of sleeping the rest of the trip away was beginning to appeal to her, but bad memories played out behind her eyelids.

"Thank you for fitting me in at such late notice," she says.

"No worries, Katie." He smiles and touches her arm. "Please, come

in." He holds the door open like the gentleman he always portrays in class.

"Thank you." She cringes at the repetition as she accepts the invite and crosses the threshold.

"Just drop you bag there and go through to the living room." He indicates a door on the left as he heads towards the kitchen. "I'll get us a drink."

She follows his directions and enters a room that surprises her. The modern furnishings and décor is not what she was expecting. He has always come across as the studious type and yet here she can't see a single book.

She passes her gaze around the room and relaxes a little. He may not be that different to her normal friends. She carries the books she has brought and makes her way over to the leather sofa. He hasn't returned yet and she takes a seat to await his return.

"I hope you like red." He enters the room holding two fluted wine glasses filled with dark liquid.

He takes a seat next to her, his knee making contact with hers. He passes her the glass and as she takes it from him their fingers brush against each other. She pays this no attention.

She is here to learn.

The evening progresses quickly and the wine is drunk as learning is pushed to one side in favour of general chat, nothing of particular importance. As time passes he moves closer, occasionally touching her arm when he explains things to her. She doesn't complain. This is a side of him she has never seen and it intrigues her.

He leaves for a moment and low music suddenly fills the room. He reappears with a second bottle of wine, the cork removed and ready to pour.

He asks her about her likes and dislikes. She replies without pause, releasing information she'd never have dreamed of giving him in the world of classrooms and lecture halls.

His next touch is lingering, his fingers resting on her knee. She notices the difference in this caress and she shifts her position. She may have consumed three glasses of alcohol, but she is immediately on guard as the atmosphere between them changes.

"What's wrong?" He moves nearer, once again placing a hand on her leg, this time above the knee.

"Nothing," she insists, yet stands up, feigning interest in the artwork above the fireplace.

"You are having fun?" he asks and she flinches as he moves up behind her.

"I think I should go now." She places the unfinished drink on the mantle and makes to leave.

"Not yet." He grabs her wrist and spins her to face him. "The night is young." His voice has taken on a menacing edge and his eyes have lost their original softness.

"I really must go." She tries to pull free, but his grip only becomes tighter.

"I said not yet," he snarls, his free hand snapping upwards and backhanding her across the cheek.

Katie awoke with a start, the van jolting her body as it hit a divot in the road. The dream-like memory of that night faded, but it would always be with her, locked away in that secret place.

"Where are we?" she asked as the van rocked again.

"Somewhere," replied Curt, his jovial tone tinged with an underlying stress. "I think I took a wrong turn." It was his way of admitting that they were, indeed, lost.

"But things may look up pretty soon," announced Josh from his crouched position between driver and passenger.

"Don't fucking start," warned Curt.

"No, seriously." Josh held up a hand in defence. "Look." He pointed. "I think I see salvation.

It stood out above the tree line like a sign from God.

TEXACO

BLACKWOOD 1999

The house hasn't had electricity for years, but this doesn't matter. The kitchen range is wood fuelled and he has wood in abundance.

He stokes it up and waits for the heat to reach a suitable temperature, listening as his guest shuffles around upstairs. She stopped screaming a while ago. It could have been hours since he last heard her, but he wouldn't know for sure. He has no need for time. All he needs to know is day and night and even that doesn't matter much anymore.

It used to when he would visit the village, but they have all gone now. Moved on to pastures new and left him in peace to live his life how he wants. They had feared him and to keep him away they had fed him, but behind closed doors he'd heard them. He had listened to their cruel words through open windows. He had endured their taunts and name calling.

HAMMERHEAD

This is the only name he remembers now. He is sure that Father named him something else, but Hammerhead is his name now. And it suits him well.

He pushes away the memories and returns his attention to the job at hand, placing his fingers on the hotplate, happy with the fizzle of fingertips and the burnt bacon aroma of singed flesh.

It's time to begin.

He takes a pan filled with brackish water from the sink and shakes it semi-dry; there is no need to clean it. The old food that clings to the side will just help add flavour to the dish he is about to prepare.

He drops the pan onto the cluttered worktop, shifting through the miasma of uneaten, rancid meals and utensils of his trade until he finds a knife. The blade is caked with rust like stains, but it will do the job well enough.

From a hessian bag he takes potatoes first and then delves deeper for the mildew covered carrots. These are cut with expert speed into thick slices and dropped in the bottom of the pan. He takes a wide brimmed jar from the windowsill and, with two dirt-encrusted fingers, he scoops out a lump of lard-like fat. This is flicked into the pan along with the vegetables. The pan is placed on the hotplate and within seconds the fat begins to fry noisily. From another jar, he pours a viscous sauce of red, so dark it is almost black, then stirs the ingredients with a broken spoon.

All it needs now is that something extra to fill it out. He takes the knife and turns slowly, as the cattle at the table renews its struggle to escape its bonds.

He looks at it, tilting his head from side to side as if deep in thought. The cattle tries to plead but the words are muffled by the gag that is tied tightly around its head.

With the knife in one hand he approaches, raising a finger to his masked face. "Ssshhh." He steps closer and the cattle renews its fight against the barbed wire that holds its wrists in place. He steps around the chair and waits patiently for the struggling to subside.

The cattle cries, tears of fear falling down its cheeks and soaking the already moist gag. Finally, through exhaustion it slumps in the seat. All the fight has gone, the spirit is already dead.

He reaches forward, taking a handful of the cattle's hair and yanks the head back. The knife slices with ease, cutting deep into the tear stained cheek. He works quickly and savagely as the cattle kicks out at the floor in desperate agony, still alive as the flesh is peeled from the bone. He cuts away strips and drops them on the table. Only when he has enough will he take it to the pan. Once he has taken all the choice fillets from the face, he moves onto the chest, carving larger sections as the cattle finally loses its grip on life.

When he has a decent pile of varied sized chunks and slices, he scoops them up in his apron and carries them across to the pan, shaking the meat into the boiling stew.

Happy with the feast, he leaves it to cook, but before leaving the kitchen to fetch his guest, he drags the chair and its cargo of half filleted carcass into the corner and throws an old coat over the mess.

There is no need to disturb his guest unnecessarily. He's hoping to keep this one for a while.

He misses having a mother around.

He moves out of the kitchen and into the hallway, pausing at the bottom of the stairs to listen. She's been very quiet, which is good. He likes them to behave. Then he doesn't have to punish them. They're never the same after being punished. It always leaves them limp and cold.

He hopes this one is good. She is so pretty and he likes the way she smells. Under the fear he has picked up on her sweetness. He can't understand why, but he feels that this one is special. Maybe he will be able to do the things to her that Father used to force him to do with the other Mothers.

The house isn't quite what it used to be and he has to take the stairs carefully. If Father was still around things would have been better looked after. He doesn't have time for such ventures and so everything has fallen into a state of disrepair.

He doesn't mind. He likes things the way they are but, if the new mother settles in, he might try and get some jobs done around the old place. The thought makes him chuckle.

The upstairs is darker than the ground floor. The windows have been boarded up since Father's time. The planks are now old and rotten. Thin beams of sunlight creep in through the gaps, but are quickly eaten up by the darkness of the house.

He moves with a purpose along the landing; it's a journey he's made many times and he doesn't need to look for the loose floorboards. Their placement is etched in memory.

The door is locked from the outside and the key resists as he turns it, opening the bolt with a screech and a snap. Before he even opens the door he knows that something is wrong.

Her scent has changed.

He pushes the door open and looks at his guest and his anger flares.

Her eyes bulge from her purple face, the electrical cord having dug deeply into her neck. Her feet sway above the floor, one shoe kicked free as she twitched her last.

He screams and thrashes out at the body, tearing at the clothes and flesh with rampant ferociousness. He beats at the corpse as he curses her

in a voice nobody could understand.
She was supposed to be good.

CHAPTER THREE

The groups spirits had been lifted with the sight of the banner announcing the petrol station, but they quickly started to drop again as they rounded the next bend in the road.

The sign should have read:

Welcome to blackwood
Drive carefully

However, amateurish hands had defaced the weathered board. The flaking words now read:

HELL IS BLACKWOOD
JUST DRIVE CAR

Scrawled below in rushed handwriting, someone had added the warning:

DO NOT FEED THE HAMMERHEAD

"I've no intention of giving anything away to the local wildlife," muttered Curt as he slowed down for the next bend.

"What's a hammerhead?" asked Judy. "It's a kind of bear, ain't it?"

Josh laughed. "Bear!" He couldn't believe what he'd just heard come out of her mouth. "It's a kind of shark, you dumb bitch." The remark was meant to be light hearted.

"And when was the last time you saw a fucking shark in the woods?" Judy yelled back. "Now who's a dumb bitch?"

"Will you two knock it off," Katie snapped at them. "It's like listening to a couple of kids."

"Think of it as practice for when you drop the young one."

Josh leaned over and reached out to tap her motherly lump.

"Fuck off." Katie batted his hand away. "You're worse than a child."

"Listen to the grown up," sniped Judy, forgetting that Josh had started it all and siding with him.

"All of you shut it now!" Curt slammed on the brakes and the van jolted to a stop on the blind side of the bend. "One more word and you'll be walking the rest of the way." The engine stuttered and died.

The arguing stopped and Josh bit back on what he wanted to say. He knew when he'd gone too far and this was just another of those times. Curt waited for a smart comeback and, when he was happy that one wasn't forthcoming, he restarted the Shag Wagon, relieved that it worked the first time. He wouldn't be able to handle a break down. His nerves were shredded and all he wanted to do was fill up with petrol, then find the main road.

No one spoke as he negotiated the next couple of tight bends that almost brought them back on themselves but, as he rounded the last one and left the claustrophobia of the trees behind, Curt broke the silence.

"Cunt," he cursed, slamming his palm against the steering wheel. "This can't be fucking happening."

"I warned you about the Hills Have Eyes," Josh mumbled in the back.

As Curt slowed and came to a stop, they all looked through the windscreen at the boarded up petrol station.

"So, this is Blackwood," guessed Judy, unimpressed by what she saw.

It wasn't only the fuel depot that was closed. It was clear to see that once upon a time Blackwood had been a pleasant little village tucked away in the English countryside. It had been a single road Hamlet of old cottages and a couple of newer houses that sat in-between them, but even these had been built to match the feel of the rest of the place. The only truly modern looking structure was the garage, a metal unit erected on the very outer edge of Blackwood.

"Well," groaned Katie. "What now?"

"I don't know about you lot," Judy answered. "But I need to stretch my legs." She had a small battle with the door handle before it clunked open and she jump down.

"She's right," added Josh. "We may as well look around whilst we're here." He grabbed his bag and rummaged about inside. "I'm going to get some pictures of the old place."

"What a waste of fucking time." Curt was tapping the dashboard impatiently. "I'm going to see if any of the pumps are working." He threw the driver's side door open bad-temperedly. "You never know."

"Don't hold your breath," said Katie, climbing out behind Josh.

"I won't." Curt looked over at the petrol station and shook his head.

Josh was already heading away down the uneven road and eyeing up the ghost-like houses. He would get some great shots for the project he was working on. The light was just right, casting shadows over the decrepit structures and giving them the look of giant tombstones. Each one was an epitaph to the families who had once lived there.

"I wonder where they all went." Katie had joined him.

"God knows, but they must have left in a hurry." Josh pointed at the front garden of the nearest house.

"That's creepy." Katie shivered.

"Creepy?" Josh disagreed. "It's perfect." He dragged her along as he readied the camera.

The box of children's toys had been left on its side, the contents spilling out over the brown, patchy front lawn. Josh wasted no time in crouching down and framing the shot, ensuring that he kept the aged front of the cottage in the background. He snapped away as he moved around, taking a dozen pictures from different angles.

"What about the tricycle?" Katie pointed it out.

"Thanks. You might have an eye for this after all." Josh left the box of playthings and walked over to the kid's three wheeled bike, kicking it over before raising the camera.

"What did you do that for?" Katie asked in dismay.

"It adds to the sense of loss," replied Josh matter of factly.

"Oh." The sight of the toys made her sad. "My baby will have everything it wants and more," she said out of the blue, holding her stomach protectively.

"It sure will." Josh lowered the camera and walked over to her, putting an arm around her shoulders. "And imagine the fun he'll have with a Godfather like me."

"For starters, who said it's a boy?" Katie shrugged his arm away and playfully elbowed his ribs. "And who said you were being nominated as Godfather?"

"I nominated myself," answered Josh, replacing the arm and pulling her close. "I know I rile you up sometimes, but I'll always be there for you."

"Thanks." Katie then surprised herself and kissed him on the cheek. "You tell the others I just did that and I'll kill you," she laughed.

It felt good to laugh; she'd not done enough of it since becoming pregnant. Being with friends and away from the learning environment was helping her to relax. She promised herself to do it more often.

"Come on," urged Josh. "Let's take a look inside."

"I'm not sure about that." Katie looked at the house and a cold shiver ran up her spine. "It's probably locked anyway."

"Only one way to find out."

Curt walked away from the van, knowing that the petrol station was already a no brainer. He should have listened to Katie and headed back to the main road when they first realised they were going the wrong way. He hated letting the others down and he blamed himself for the way things were turning out. He just hoped that the beach house would make up for it all. The thought of reaching the coast managed to bring a smile to his face. Regardless of how bad the trip was, the holiday was going to rock. All they had to do was get there.

He reached the small forecourt and walked across the cracked tarmac, kicking at the weeds that had broken through in search of sunlight. He headed for the main building first. The windows were boarded up, but the door had been untouched. If they were lucky someone still worked here, a lone employee paid to sit around all day and help out those who had decided to go the wrong way.

"Yeah and I've got a chance with Judy," he berated himself as he nudged the screen door open with his foot, pausing to look over his shoulder.

Judy was still pacing up and down alongside of the van, swinging her arms from side to side. He watched her for a moment and then turned his gaze towards Katie and Josh. They were standing in front of one of the old houses, considering whether to enter or not. Josh was nodding and smiling, but Katie didn't seem as eager.

Josh left them to it and stepped out of the afternoon sun. The inside was as dingy and silent just as he'd known it would be. The shop area had been left as it must have been on the last day of business. The shelves were still full and a magazine rack displayed row upon row of magazines.

"Bizarre," whispered Curt, letting the door swing closed behind him as he ventured deeper.

Judy saw Curt looking at her, but she didn't let on. She knew he had a thing for her and, if she told the truth, she liked him more than he'd ever realise. She was hoping the trip would be the ideal place for her to broach the subject with him. She watched him from the corner of her eye and smiled to herself. Sometimes he was a real pain in the arse, but underneath it all she was sure she would find that little something extra. It also helped that she found him gorgeous to look at, his dark eyes and darker hair gave him an exotic air. She'd talked about this with Katie the night before and her friend had told her to go for it.

"I will," she said to herself, "but now's not the right time." She was still watching him as he disappeared inside the rusted metal building. "Maybe before we set off again..."

That idea was quickly ruined by the scream.

Curt came running out of the petrol station. The door exploded from the frame as he rammed through it. The hinges, weak with age, gave under the pressure and he fell to one side. He'd heard the scream as he leafed through a seven-year-old edition of the TV guide and recognized it immediately as having come from Katie.

As he left the forecourt, he turned his head and saw Judy dashing to catch him up. Without breaking stride, he pointed at her. "Stay near the van," he shouted between deep breaths.

"It was Katie!" Judy yelled, tears already filling her eyes.

"I know!" yelled Curt over his shoulder. "Just get in the van."

He left the road and hurdled the fence, landing on the box of toys and falling forward. Pain shot up his left leg as his knee smashed against the crazy paved pathway.

"Curt!" It was Judy.

"Van!" he yelled angrily. "Now!"

Curt untangled himself from the action figures and dressing up outfits and limped into the house.

"Katie, Josh!"

"We're in here," yelled Josh from the rear of the house.

Curt slowed as he entered the hallway. The walls were caked in brownish smears and the place stank like shit. Before continuing he pulled his t-shirt up over his nose. He trod carefully as he progressed, realising that the marks on the walls were more than just smears. Whatever coated the walls had been used as ink and the words had been painted in tall words that reached from floor to ceiling.

BEWARE THE HAMMER

The warning covered nearly the entire length of the wall.

YOUNG AND FRESH IS ALWAYS BEST

"What the fuck is going on?" Curt shouted through his t-shirt and his hand.

"We have a slight problem back here," Josh replied. "Could do with a little help."

Curt slid and looked down, dismayed to find his foot imbedded in a puddle of yellowish, liquid turd. The sole of his shoe had broken the filmy skin of the surface and the smell hit him like a wall of crap.

"Fucking hell," he gagged.

"Oh, and watch your step," added Josh. "Our new friend likes to play with his own mess."

"Just figured that one out." Curt did his best to breath through his mouth as he wiped the shit from his shoe on the damp carpet.

"Could you hurry up?" Katie requested, a slight hint of giggle mixed with her concern.

"Just give me a minute." Curt watched the floor as he manoeuvred through the remaining minefield of human faeces.

Josh and Katie were standing side by side, big smiles on their faces. They turned to look at Curt as he stepped into the kitchen.

"Glad you could make it," Josh said, trying his hardest to keep a straight face.

"What happened?" asked Curt.

"He did," replied Katie pointing to the corner of the room.

Curt peered around the edge and discovered the owner of the house and the shit-based graffiti.

"I think he's harmless," Josh stated, "but he scared Katie."

"Scared me," she complained. "I pissed myself."

At that moment, Josh couldn't hold back any longer and started to laugh.

"Shut up," the owner screamed at them, his face turning red and the veins in his neck threatening to rupture. "He'll hear you," he hissed the warning.

"You're nuts, mate," Josh said.

"He can smell fresh meat." The owner stood up and Katie yelped in surprise.

In one hand, the man held a bucket that was filled to the brim with steaming shit. He thrust a hand in the bucket and walked towards them.

"Cover your scent or he'll find you." He stepped towards them. "He likes them young and pretty."

"Who does?" Katie stammered.

"Can't say his name," the owner whispered, his eyes flicking around the room.

"The hammerhead?" guessed Josh.

"Don't say his name." the man screamed, dropping the bucket and clamping his crap-covered hands over his ears. "Don't say his name." He spun to face the wall and began to beat his head against the bare brickwork.

"Don't say his name." Between each head butt he repeated the mantra. "Don't say his name."

"Josh, get Katie back to the van," Curt snapped as fear crept into his gut.

"You can't leave now," The owner of the house faced them with wild eyes. "He'll find you and put you in his stewing pot," he screamed at them as pulled the knife from his waistband.

"Josh," urged Curt, but his friends were already moving.

Josh pushed Katie in front and they ran down the hallway, no longer worried about what they might tread in. There were worse things than shit on their shoes to worry about. Curt followed close behind, slamming the kitchen door shut in the owner's face.

"Run."

"No need to tell us," replied Josh, any humour the situation may have held now replaced by seriousness.

"He'll find you." The owner's veins stood out on his neck as he burst into the hallway, waving the knife above his head. "Let me save you."

"Fuck you," shouted Josh as he shoved Katie out into the fresh air of the afternoon.

Curt wasn't far behind them and he snatched hold of Katie's wrist. "Move." She held her stomach as she tried to keep up with him.

Judy saw them coming and opened the side door, helping a breathless Katie into the back as Curt ran around and jumped behind the wheel.

"Young and fresh is always best!" The owner of the house rushed out to find them, the knife in one hand and the bucket of human waste in the other.

"He'll put you in his stewing pot!" He took scoops of the brown matter and flung it at the van as the engine fired up with complaint.

"Get in, Judy," Josh dragged her into the back and slid the door shut as Curt ground the gears into first and pulled forward.

"Young and fresh!" screamed the shit flinger as he jumped in front of the van.

"Fuck." Curt tried to swerve, but it was too late.

The thump of skull hitting windscreen was sickening, but Curt didn't stop. He moved up to second gear and carried on driving.

"You killed him," Judy sobbed.

"I ain't going back to find out." As he put the van into third his hands shook. "Now give me the map and let's find a main road."

"But you killed him," repeated Judy.

"This never happened," he shouted at her. "Do you understand? Never happened." The look in her eyes broke his heart, but there was no way he was going back now.

BLACKWOOD 1999

He has to work harder for his meat now; it's not as easy as when the villagers were here. They used to leave him food in the barn, an unspoken agreement where they helped feed him and he didn't feed on them. It was a long running arrangement, started long before he was born and it had suited the family. But that all stopped on they day they left.

Even the one who stinks, the one who remained behind when the others left has stopped with his deliveries of fruit and vegetables. Not that they were ever friends. Hammerhead doesn't have friends; it's not in his nature. Still, sometimes it felt good to know that someone else was out there.

Things are different now, changing slowly with each turning of the seasons. It has made his way of life harder and now he must hunt more during the summer if he is to survive the winter. Sometimes he wishes that Father hadn't left. Life would have been different; more painful and laden with beatings, but different nonetheless.

He has worked hard this summer, the hunts have been far more frequent and the prey appears to be better fed than in previous years. This has made him happy as he gets to bottle more lard for cooking. Yes, he has worked hard, and the cold store in the basement is full to bursting. The cattle is all butchered ready for future consumption and now it is time to clean house again.

He starts with the smaller bins of waste. He's utilised everything he can and the rest is of no use. He started the bonfire earlier and it is burning well, hot enough for the greedy flames to eat away at the raw fuel. He empties the bins one and a time, pausing between each one to listen to the snap, crackle and pop of frying skin and cartilage.

He quickly moves on to the larger barrels, rolling them one at a time out of the back door. They are full and he struggles with the uneven load, the thick liquid within slopping over the edges and covering his lower arms. After the fourth barrel he is tired, yet nowhere near finished. His stomach is grumbling with hunger, the haunting fragrance of char-grilled offal causing him to salivate.

He answers the call by fishing into the nearest barrel and swishing his arm around in the treacle-like fluid. He grunts with satisfaction as his fingers entwine in matted hair. He lifts the severed head free of the barrel and shakes the weeks-old blood from it as much as he can. Not that rancid meat will ever put him off. It's never made him sick yet. To him, it is all sustenance, a quick snack to tide him over until later.

He sits down on the back step with a sigh of relief, shifting until the pain in his back eases somewhat. He holds the head in one hand and pushes a finger down between the left eye and the socket. The flesh is soft, pliable and surprisingly warm to the touch. He forces the finger deeper, hooking it behind the orb and then plucking it free. He shoves it in his mouth and bites down. Age and decay has given the usually salty dish a sour flavour and he allows the rank liquid to sit on his tongue before swallowing. The right eye goes down just as easy.

He likes the eyes. He has an almost forgotten memory of being told that the eyes are the gateway to the soul. Not that it means anything to him now; he just likes the taste and the feel as they dissolve in his mouth.

As he swallows the second eye he turns the head in his hands and watches as maggots squirm in the festering wound where the neck has been severed. Without hesitating he lifts it to his mouth and sinks his teeth into the rotten flesh, tearing a chunk away with hungry abandon. His stomach screams for more and he replies by gorging himself on rank flesh and fly larva, devouring the neck meat and then moving onto the face.

He leaves the ears till last, ripping them from the head and shoving them in his pocket. He'll save them for later. They don't taste of much, but they're chewy and gristly. He'll have them later in the afternoon.

He drops what is left of the head back into the barrel. It bobs on the surface for a few short seconds, spinning until the face sinks from sight and then it sinks with a bubbling fart. The sound makes him laugh; a mucus-filled chuckle that causes pink tinted spit to run over the lips of his mask and down the chin.

He stops laughing, as he notices the fire is burning low and the day is moving on. It's time to finish up before he loses the afternoon light. There is much to do and only him to do it.

He rolls the first barrel across the garden – not that anyone would ever call the overgrown tangle of weeds and brambles a garden. His breathing comes in moist pant-like wheezes as he struggles to keep the barrel balanced.

Cleaning house gets harder every year.

He continues to fight with his load until he reaches the waist-high ferns that surround the house and then pauses for breath. Usually he would go further, but today he is feeling lazy and unsettled. The discovery of the new mother hanging from the bedroom ceiling has left him feeling sad and his heart just isn't in the work at hand.

He kicks the barrel over with a heavy grunt, the contents pouring into the undergrowth with a momentary tidal wave of tar-like blood and bodily remains. Not everything is washed away and he takes a few moments to kick the unrecognisable lumps out of sight.

Father always kept a clean house.

He works slowly as the afternoon turns into evening, finishing the barrels before moving onto the sacks that line the hallway and landing. He's collected a decent hoard of goodies this year and shouldn't have to worry too much about going hungry during the colder months.

Tomorrow he will venture out into the woods and lay his snares regardless. You can never have too much meat stored away and a couple of rabbits will come in useful for breakfasts and suppers.

The sky is turning dark as he reaches completion. He has only one thing left to dispose of and that is the new mother. She is no longer hanging in the bedroom, her body and head having come apart when he beat her corpse so savagely for misbehaving.

Since then he has laid her out on the kitchen table. He had planned on adding her to the store, but for some reason he can't bring himself to butcher her like the others. She is still very pretty and her dead eyes look up at him from the table.

He wants to keep her around for a while, look after her and care for her. He wants to keep her warm on a night, but it's too late for that. She is beyond warmth; she belongs to the cold now.

He lifts the body and places it over his shoulder and picks up the head by the long, blonde hair. As he leaves the house he hums a tune that he no longer remembers, the tone and rhythm all wrong.

He moves slowly out into the ferns this time; she isn't a waste object to be thrown away. For some unexplainable reason she is special. He takes her into the centre of his graveyard, a place reserved for all the other mothers he has had over the years. He is careful not to stand on them, striding over bodies that vary in their state of decay.

Only when he finds a suitable spot does he lay the body down, taking care to ensure she will be comfortable. In his own way, he is trying to say sorry for hurting her. This isn't how it should have been. He places her arms next to her side and tries his best to straighten her tattered clothing. When he is satisfied, he stands up and holds the head in front of his own. The eyes are still open and he searches them for something he doesn't understand.

Could it be love? Could it be acceptance? He will never know. He left that kind of humanity behind him long ago.

He draws the head close and tilts his own to one side, pulling her lips to his. She feels cool against his warmth as he kisses her. As he grinds their lips together he stares into her blank eyes.

He can feel tears running down his cheeks, something he hasn't done since Father was around. Back then he would cry on a regular basis. The whippings and the mental abuse at his parent's hands had been insufferable. But he had learned to live with it. It had made him the man that he is and he knows Father would be proud. He realises as he pulls the head back that this one looks like his first mother, his real mother. They have the same colour eyes in death.

His tears come harder as he pictures blurred images of mother and how she had looked after her punishment. Father had warned her about playing with the cattle, but she hadn't listened. Father had been forced to teach her a lesson.

He screams at the memory of his mother and how she had felt under him that last time. He kisses the head on each cheek and then places it as best he can atop the neck.

Only then does he begin to undress.

FOUR

The engine began to judder not far outside of the ghost town known as Blackwood. Curt looked down at the petrol gauge with dismay. It had been hovering around empty for nearly an hour and now the needle had dropped below the big 'E'.

He pumped the accelerator in a last ditch attempt to draw any reserves forward, but it was a useless exercise. Before it had a chance to croak its last, he pulled off the road and on to the wide grass verge. As Curt yanked on the handbrake the exhaust let out a huge black cloud and a final, spluttering fart.

"Fuck it," he snarled, removing the seatbelt. "Fuck it," he repeated as he flung the door open angrily and stepped out onto the roadside.

"What now?" Josh asked as he came around from a restless sleep.

"Fuck it," ranted Curt, lashing out at the front wing with his foot. "Fuck it." Pain flared in his ankle as the kick made an awkward impact.

"We killed a man," replied Judy.

"Fuck it," was all that Curt could manage as he hopped on one leg and massaged the other. "Fuck it, fuck it, and fuck it."

"So," Katie squeezed between the two front seats, "apart from fucking it, what else do we do now?" She went for the breezy approach, not caring to admit that they were in pretty deep shit. That could and would come later; for now they had to think about helping themselves.

She manoeuvred herself into the driver's seat and took the map from its screwed up place in the door compartment, straightening it out on her lap. She quickly found the black dot that marked Blackwood and then picked out the road she hoped they were now on. From there she made an attempt to judge where and how far away the next petrol station would be.

One of them would have to go on foot but anything was better than jumping around and swearing like a kid who wasn't getting his own way. Curt was a long time friend, but he had a lot of growing up to do. If he wasn't ready to take control then it would have to be down to the ladies. Well, lady.

"Curt, have we got a petrol can?" Katie looked up from the map.

"Yeah, it's in the back of the van," Curt replied, sat on the grass and carefully removing his shoe.

"Judy." Katie rested a hand on the other girl's knee. "You're coming with me."

"Where are we going?"

"I think there's a petrol station about two hours from here." She rechecked the map and nodded. "Once we're there, we can ring for a taxi to bring us back."

"That's it," Josh sat up straight and started searching his bag. "We'll ring someone." He held up the mobile phone like a trophy.

"No point," Katie stated. "There's no signal out here."

"Fucking great," groaned Josh, holding down the power button and waiting for the phone to come to life.

"I'll go with Judy," said Curt, rubbing his ankle as he circled his foot.

"I'm more than capable of walking a few miles," Katie took a defensive stance.

"Yeah, but you're also pregnant." Curt looked up at her from his position on the ground. "What if something happens with the baby?" He raised his eyebrows. "You're better off here with Josh."

Curt waited for a reply, smiling with satisfaction as Katie nodded.

"That's settled then." Curt pulled on his shoe and began tying the laces. "Katie, give me your phone and as soon as I get a signal I'll ring your mum and let her know we'll be late." He held out his hand. "No point having everyone worrying about us."

"Thanks," said Katie, throwing the useless mobile over to him.

"I'm not going anywhere with him," Judy sneered. "He should have stopped to help that man."

"He had a fucking knife, Judy," Curt explained. "He could have hurt you." He blushed slightly at his show of manly concern.

"You killed him."

"We don't know that for sure," added Katie. "And if you go with Curt you can ring for an ambulance as soon as the phone works."

The idea appealed to Judy and she offered a sad looking smile.

"I'll have to get changed first." Judy stood and climbed into the back. "It's starting to get chilly."

"Good idea." Curt tried to hide his pleasure at getting a chance to spend some time with Judy. "I'll need a coat."

He may have blown it with his actions earlier, but now he had a couple of hours to try and make it up to her. He didn't want this to be the end of the holiday. He got up and limped around the van. His knee was still throbbing, and kicking the van had jarred his ankle. The walk was going to be painful but worth it if he could be with Judy.

"I'll give you two some privacy," Josh said, sliding open the side door and jumping out as Curt pulled himself up.

Katie got out of the front, taking the map with her and triple checking her estimations. She just hoped that Judy and Curt could work out their differences. The events of the day had left them both strung out, but it was as clear as day that both had a thing for each other. She knew it, Josh knew it. Hell, everybody back at the University knew it. It wouldn't be easy, but things would be better if they could get over it and admit their feelings.

Curt rummaged through the bags. He wanted his coat but, most importantly, he needed more papers for a joint. He was stressed out and needed the light-headed relief of a smoke. As he searched, he glanced over his shoulder and saw Judy slipping off her T shirt. He followed the curve of her stomach up to the small, yet pert breasts held within the confines of her turquoise bra. He couldn't believe how beautiful she was and he suddenly needed to tell her.

But first he needed that joint. He found the carrier bag he'd filled with such essentials and pulled out a fresh packet of papers and set to work on rolling a smoke.

"Why didn't you stop?" Judy asked without warning.

"I was scared," replied Curt, mixing the sage green coloured weed with dark brown tobacco.

"You? Scared?" She didn't sound convinced.

"I heard the scream and I thought you were hurt."

"I didn't realise you cared." She frowned, not believing the line of excuse he was taking.

"Well I do care," he snapped a little harsher than he'd wanted to. "I've cared for quite a while now."

"Oh." Judy finally saw the truth of what he was saying and the revelation came as somewhat of a shock. "You should have said something."

"I tried, but we're mates and I didn't want to look like an idiot." Curt had wanted to smoke the joint before this discussion and he was quickly growing embarrassed.

"So you killed a man to prove your love?" The sarcastic comment was accompanied by a small smile.

"I just panicked and I feel worse about it than you do." With shaking hands he lit the joint and inhaled deeply. "I've got to live the fact that I drove off." From the corner of his eye a tear formed and he turned to find his coat before Judy saw he was crying.

"We'll sort it out together," Judy said softly.

Curt heard her moving and kept his back to her as he tried to hold back the tears.

Curt found his coat, but kept pretending to search as he wiped his eyes with his arm. He couldn't let Judy see just how weak he felt. He wanted her to feel secure when they were together. He continued looking until he saw the petrol can and heaved it up from under the pile of bags and supplies.

"Right, I'm ready," Judy said and went to pull open the door.

"Wait." Curt turned and stepped over to her.

He wanted to slip an arm around her shoulder and pull her too him. Instead he said. "We need a torch."

"Come on, you two." Josh thumped the side of the van. "It'll be midnight before you get back at this rate."

"Fuck off, Josh," Curt shouted back as he found the torch amongst the other junk he'd piled in at the start of the day. He smiled at Judy as he leaned passed her and took hold of the handle. "Or we'll book into a hotel for the night and leave you out here in the cold and dark."

"That's OK by me," Josh fired back. "I've got Katie to keep me warm." He grinned up at Curt as the door slid back to reveal them.

"In your dreams." Katie looked up. "Curt, take a look at this before you leave." She waved the now tattered looking map.

"Yes, Madam." Curt saluted as he jumped down, flinching as a red hot poker of pain flared up his leg. "Wouldn't want us getting lost."

"Again," Josh laughed.

"I've warned you once." Curt pointed at him.

Katie walked over to the front of the van and spread the map out so that Curt could see what she had planned for him.

"I think we're about here," Katie explained, placing her finger on the narrow white line that indicated the road out of Blackwood. "Carry on to this point." She traced a line up to where the road intersected with a yellow coloured one. "Then it's straight up to Scarthwell." As she spoke, Curt nodded. "They should have a petrol station and at the least you'll be able to get to a phone and send someone out to get us."

Curt frowned, concentrating on the map before deciding to say anything.

"We could just cut across at this point and save time,"

he suggested, running a finger in a diagonal between the intersection and Scarthwell.

"That's not the best idea," Katie disagreed. "It'll be getting dark soon and you'd be safer on the roads." She folded the map and gave it to Curt. "Then, if a car passes you'll see it."

"More importantly," Judy added, "they'll see us."

"Whatever," said Curt, forcing the map into his jacket pocket. "We'll sort it out on the way."

"Don't stray from the path," Josh screeched. "The Hammerhead will get you."

"Josh you're a fucking idiot." Judy shivered. "We'll stick to the roads." She took Curt's hand and started walking.

"Don't forget to text my mum if you get a signal," Katie shouted after them.

"You're in safe hands," Curt replied. "Josh will look after you."

That wasn't the most comforting of thoughts and Katie flicked him the middle finger.

BLACKWOOD – PRESENT DAY

It has been a bad year for the Hammerhead. The hunt has been harder than usual and the prey is becoming scarcer with every passing season. He can remember a time when the cattle could be found and stalked on a daily basis. Back then he could stock up well for the winter and never fear of going hungry.

The last season was just as poor and if it hadn't been for the cattle he'd found wandering through the woods he would have starved. It had been a good hunt, only one adult in the herd, the rest still only young and subtle. He had followed them for hours as they had travelled deeper and deeper into the woods, all dressed in matching clothing. He'd waited until night and then he had taken the adult first. He had been easy, no fight in him at all. It had taken only one blow to the temple and the kill had been done. He'd dragged the body home and hung it in the basement by its ankles, slitting the throat and letting the corpse slowly bleed into an old tin bucket.

The young ones of the herd had been even easier; he'd only had to slaughter a few of them before the others had come willingly. He'd been able to keep many of them alive, tied up in the old barn and feeding them on leftovers until he needed them. It had been a good winter of sweet meat, but that had been down to pure luck. It wouldn't happen this year.

No, this year he is being forced to do something he hasn't done in an age. If he wants to feed he must scavenge. It disgusts him to drop so low; no better than a fox in the night. He is superior to the other woodland animals and this is an insult to all that Father ever taught him.

He will have to steal what he needs and for that there is only one place he can go. He hasn't been there since they all left, but, if he is to survive, concessions must be made.

He doesn't expect to have to hunt, but he was taught to be prepared for anything. With this in mind, he is armed with the tools of his trade. The belt holds everything he needs to deal with an unexpected kill and he feels better knowing that his special hammer is hanging at his waist.

As he travels towards the village, he checks on his snares. At least they have proved effective this season. He already has a wall of rabbits in the basement. They will keep him going, but they aren't the same as cattle. There is no hunting involved with the rabbits, no sense of satisfaction in skinning their dead bodies, and gutting them is an emotionless experience. Only the cattle can give him the sense of achievement that he needs.

He has already collected a good half dozen rabbits. These now hang over his shoulder; they smell rich and the fur will come in useful, yet still he dreams of having one good hunt before the cold weather settles in.

He knows that the village is near; he can smell the difference in the air. The freshness and innocence of his woodland home is tinged with aromas that mark it out as man made. He remembers a time when the scent would have been stronger; a warning to his senses to move away during the daylight hours. That had been a time when he would have waited until well past dusk before venturing into Blackwood. Even then, with the shadows of night to keep him hidden he would have remained silent as he crept between the houses and peered in on his neighbours.

He snorts a laugh at the thought of their ever having been his neighbours. To them, he had been no more than a wild animal to be avoided at all costs. To him, they had been cattle, just another link in the food chain.

Now it is different. The village is nothing more than a grave yard of hollow memories and faded smells. It's part of his world now and he can walk the street without fear of being seen. He wonders why he hasn't visited sooner. After all, it may hold many treats that he can salvage. Suddenly the thought of scavenging doesn't seem so lowly. He deserves to take something from them in return for all the years of loneliness. He's only taking what they owe him and, anyway, what use do they have of it now?

As he enters the village his good humour lifts him up and he laughs again, considering moving house. He could claim any one of these houses as his own. The old house is full of reminders of Father and the numerous mothers. He could start again with something that was just his.

It would be hard work moving the butchered cattle he does have, but he starts to consider the idea. He could own the entire village and then try and find a new family to bring home. He hasn't even attempted to try and take a new mother in quite a while, but if he lived here he could go one better and try for a wife; a mate.

The thought excites him and he begins to whoop and holler in the garbled language only he knows. He moves along the street with a lightness to his step, unwary of who may see him. Then he stops and sniffs the air nosily. He can smell cattle blood and something else. Once again he becomes the stealthy hunter, his eyes darting from left to right as he follows his nose.

The scent of blood is strong, but underneath he picks up on other aromas. He recognises one as the foul stench of the smelly one that used to feed him on occasion. He hopes he is still here. He feels like having fun and nothing comes close to dealing out punishment on those who have asked for it.

He sees the pool of blood and kneels down, dipping his fingers into the precious liquid. It's still warm and this excites him, the other scents he has picked up on are quickly forgotten as his hunters instinct comes to the fore. He places the red coated fingers to his masked lips and tastes the coppery flavour. It is, indeed, as fresh as the touch had suggested.

He drops down on all fours and laps up the puddle greedily, the tangy flavour of life force sparking his hunger and heightening his senses. He slurps until there is no more to have, scraping his stump of a tongue sore on the roughened tarmac of the road surface. Only then does he look around as he smells the ground. He has the scent fixed in his mind and he searches the floor around him for signs. The trail of blood is not hard to find and he uses it as a guide, remaining on all fours and licking up every last droplet as he follows the red markers.

He crawls faster as he leaves the road and enters the garden of a house he watched many a time when it was inhabited by cattle. The scent of the stinky one is stronger here, but he is only interested in the punishment ahead. He finally stands upright and enters the house, breathing deep of the shit and blood that fills his nostrils.

He can hear the laboured breathing from the back of the house.

"I know you're there," says the stinky one. "You don't want me."

He listens to the voice as he walks along the hallway, withdrawing the hammer from its place at his waist.

"Young and fresh is best," sings the stinky one between rasping breaths. "Young and fresh."

He walks along the pathway of smeared excrement at his feet, the putrefied brown smeared with deep red. The stinky one is injured and this lessens the value of the hunt.

He enters the kitchen and sees the trail lead out of the back door. Injured or not, the stinky one tries to escape. He studies the kitchen for a moment, deciding that this is not the house he will chose for his own. It has been violated by the stinky one and will have to be burned to the ground.

He leaves the house and steps out into the garden, a pathway of blood and shit leads the way to the shed in the corner.

Hide and seek.

He strides across the garden, ignoring the slide and the swing that had once given children so much enjoyment. He approaches the shed and then stands outside silently, listening to the stinky one sobbing within.

"Young and fresh, young and fresh," chants the stinky one, but his words are growing weaker.

He tears the door open and raises the hammer, ready to deal out his punishment. The stinky one covers his dirt encrusted face with blood soaked hands, but the blow never comes.

He looks passed the stinky one in wonder; his eyes widening at what hangs from the inner wall of the shed. Never has he seen such a toy of such magnificence. He looks at the long handle with a gaze that borders on love. He lowers the clawed hammer and pushes it back into the belt that Father gave him when he was still a child.

At his feet the stinky one whimpers, but he ignores him, reaching over the top of him and lifting down the new toy. He has never laid eyes on a sledgehammer and he is awestruck by the power that surges through him just holding it in his hands.

"Young and fresh." The stinky one lowers his hands.

He looks down at the stinky one and grunts, swinging the mighty hammer up and then down.

"YOUN…" The stinky one begins to scream before his head implodes on impact, the heavy head of the hammer embedding itself in what is left of the neck.

With a foot placed on the stinky one's shoulder he pulls the hammer free and coos with pleasure at how well it works. The trip has turned out to be well worth it, but there is other things he needs.

Without looking back he leaves the stinky one to rot, passing back through the house and back to his search for scavenged food stuff.

As he nears the vacated garage he picks up on the other aroma that was forgotten with his blood lust. His pulse increases as he realises what the other scent is.

He can smell cattle. It's not a strong scent, but they have passed through recently.

He grips the hammer to his chest and screams out with joy.

FIVE

Katie looked at her watch for the fifth time in so many minutes and tutted. Curt and Judy had only been gone an hour but she was worried about them. She knew how strong-headed Curt could be and she could only hope that he'd kept to the road as she'd suggested. She knew it would make the journey longer, but it was safer.

She glanced at the watch once again and realised she had to take her mind off them or she'd go mad. She attempted to clear her mind of the images of friends lost in the woods, focusing instead on problems closer to home. She hadn't eaten all afternoon and her stomach was rumbling. Letting herself go hungry wasn't good for her and more importantly it was bad for the baby. She had to think of the tiny life that was slowly growing inside her.

She wanted this child so much, but that hadn't always been the case. Katie cursed herself for such thoughts; she'd promised herself months ago that she wouldn't dwell on the past. The future was all that mattered. The future and her baby. She'd prove she was more than just an object. She'd show him that she was a person and that she was stronger than him.

"I'm starving," she said turning to face Josh. "What we got to eat?"

"I've got a Snickers bar," Josh replied, delving into his pack.

"I want food, not a snack," she snapped unintentionally, feeling bad as Josh looked crestfallen.

"Sorry." He smiled at her weakly and then his face lit up. "Hold on." He jumped up from his place sat in the side opening of the van and jogged around to the back.

"What?" Katie followed him, intrigued by his sudden burst of excitement.

"These old vans have a little stove in them and I'm sure I saw Curt stuff some tinned food in here." He lifted up the rear door and started throwing bags and cases onto the roadside.

"Hey, watch my stuff," Katie moaned.

"If you want to eat." Josh grinned and his happiness was catching.

"I need to eat," replied Katie and started helping with the unloading.

In no time at all, everything was out of the van and lying in unruly heaps on the grass verge. They could tidy before the others returned, but all that mattered was food.

"TADA!" announced Josh as he pulled open what appeared to be a drawer, but turned out to be a two ring, gas hob.

"Will it work?" asked Katie dubiously.

"Only one way to find out." Josh checked his pocket for a lighter. "I think the food was in the yellow back pack."

"I'll get it from over here." Katie took the bag and walked away from the van. "You can blow yourself up and I'll eat it cold," she laughed.

"O ye of little faith," Josh teased as he turned the little black knob on the front of the unit and struck the lighter above the ring.

The gas took and a tiny ring of blue fire flared to life. Josh waved Katie back over and started searching the small cupboards for a pan.

"Baked beans with sausages or spaghetti hoops with chicken nuggets?" asked Katie as she took one of each from the pack.

"Mmmmm, student food," Josh said. "Let's pig out and have both." He held up a dented cooking pot and a tin opener.

"What are we waiting for?" giggled Katie. "Let's get this gourmet feast going.

Josh opened the tin and poured both into the pan. He sat the pan on the stove and then checked another drawer, pleased to find a selection of knives and forks. He handed one of each to

Katie, holding onto his own for stirring purposes.

"I hope those two are alright." Katie looked at her watch.

"They'll be fine," reassured Josh.

"But what about that freak back in Blackwood?"

"I don't think he'll be dead, but he'll be in no fit state to follow us." Josh stirred with one hand and laid the other on Katie's shoulder.

"What about all that Hammerhead shit he was spouting?" She'd tried not to take the mad ranting seriously, but she couldn't help but be nervous.

"Katie, the bloke was out of his head," said Josh. "He'd covered himself in shit."

"But..."

"No buts," interrupted Josh. "He was a fucking nutter, but he's well behind us."

Katie nodded and managed a smile. Happy that he'd appeased her fears Josh turned back to the cooking.

"Shit," he cursed.

The gourmet feast turned out to be a lukewarm meal. The gas ran out before the mix of pasta and beans had a chance to reach boiling point. Josh didn't care, he was happy to nibble on his chicken nuggets as he watched Katie eat like she'd never seen food before.

"Here," he said. "Finish mine." He held out the chipped plate he'd found in the fold out compartment under the stove.

"Are you sure?" Katie raised an eyebrow at him.

"Yeah. I'm not that hungry."

Katie didn't give him the chance to reconsider, snatching the plate from him and scooping what was left onto her own. She hadn't realised how hungry she actually was.

"Any way, if I get peckish I've always got my Snickers bar," added Josh.

"You'd better share it," Katie said through a mouth of beans. "I'm eating for two, remember."

"Yeah, I know." Josh saw an opportunity to talk more on the

subject and he took it.

"How'd you get pregnant?"

"Well, the egg comes down the fallopian tube," Katie answered with evasion.

"No, seriously," Josh pushed the point. She hadn't spoken to anyone about the father of the child and he wanted to be there for her.

"I can't tell you." She put the plate of food down unfinished.

"Why not?" Josh knew he'd lost her.

"Just leave it."

"I want to help, that's all," he pleaded, but it was too late.

"I said leave it!" Katie shouted at him, standing up and walking away.

"Bollocks."

Katie got in the back and slammed the door shut between them, before she allowed herself to cry. She wanted to tell someone, but who would believe her. Good old Professor Reilly was one of the good guys. No one would ever dream of his doing such a thing; and if she did tell the truth, it would only cause heartache and so much more. She didn't want that. She just wanted to have her baby and live life as best she could. Maybe one day she'd be ready to talk about it, but that time wasn't now.

She peered out of the rear door, but Josh had moved away, probably in a bad mood and she couldn't blame him. He was nothing but nice to her and sometimes she felt that there could be something between them if only she tried.

BANG!

Katie screamed as the van shook, reaching out for the drivers seat as she fell forward.

"JOSH!" she screamed as the van was rocked again.

"HELP ME!" Josh yelled as something impacted with the side of the van for a third time.

"JOSH!" Katie tried to open the door, but the handle refused to budge. "JOSH!"

"HEL..." His second plea was strangled and weak.

"JOSH!" She fought with the door and it finally gave, squealing as it struggled to slide open.

"Josh," she whispered upon finding him gone.

"HAMMERHEAD!" he screamed as he jumped in to the open doorway and cracked up with laughter.

"You fucking arsehole." Katie swung a foot and kicked him in the chest.

Josh staggered backwards, tripping and landing flat on his backside with a hurt expression on his face.

"I was only playing," he insisted.

"Fucking arsehole," she snapped, closing the door and beginning to cry yet again.

"Come on, Katie," begged Josh from outside. "It was a joke."

"Wanker," she yelled back.

"Sorry."

Katie held onto the driver's seat and breathed deeply as she tried to hold the tears back. Through the windscreen she saw Josh walking towards the woods and panicked.

"Where are you going?" she yelled after him.

"I need a piss," he replied dejectedly and walked away with his head hung low.

As she watched him leave she lost the battle with her emotions and she cried. She was tired of being strong, she wanted to curl up and cry until she was empty inside. For the first time in week, she allowed herself to give in, returning to the weak child she had been on the day she found out about the baby.

The doctor sits her down and gently tells her that the Clearblue test she'd done a few days before is correct. She cries as the news tears her up from the inside out.

The doctor discusses many things with her, but she doesn't listen. Her life has already been turned upside down once and just as she is coming to terms with that she has to deal with this. Life isn't fair. How could Professor Reilly do this to her? What had she done to make him think she wanted that?

She thanks the doctor and leaves quietly. She should go straight home, but instead she returns to the house where the child was conceived in an act of violence.

She walks up the garden path and knocks on the door. She waits and then knocks again. She hears the key in the lock and the door is opened to reveal his smiling face.

"Hello Katie." He smiles as if nothing has happened.

"I'm having your baby," she states without emotion.

"Not possible, young lady." The smile never leaves his face.

"I'm having your bastard," she spits the words.

"Go away, little girl," – still he smiles – "or I'll make your life hell." He shuts the door in her face.

She wanders the streets for most of the afternoon and she cries it out of her system. She can't go home like this, so she walks until after sunset.

She ignores her flatmates as she enters, walking along the hallway and into the bathroom. She locks herself in as fresh tears run down her face.

How could this happen? University was supposed to be the start of life, not the end of it.

She runs the bath as hot as she can bear to sit in. No need for bubble bath this time, she has no intention of getting clean. She is beyond that now; she'll never be clean again.

She climbs into the scalding water, the heat of it biting at her skin as she lowers herself in. She sits for a while and the tears appear to have stopped, but she plans on stopping them forever. She snaps the razor apart and takes a single blade between thumb and forefinger. She holds the blade to her wrist with a shaking hand, but she's not strong enough to do it.

Or perhaps she is stronger than she thinks. To live will be harder than ending it all now. She has another life to think about now. It may not have been created in love, but it is more hers than it can ever be his.

At this moment her entire outlook changes.

Katie awoke with a shiver, noticing that the sky outside had faded from afternoon blue to evening purple and would very soon darken to full night black.

She was laid awkwardly in the back of the van and her left arm had gone dead. She looked around for Josh, but he wasn't there. She remembered their parting conversation as she massaged blood back into the numb limb.

"That's the longest piss in history," she said out loud.

She tried the side door, but it was jammed again and this time it refused to open. She pulled on a body warmer she'd been using as a pillow and clambered into the front of the van, flinching as pins and needles flared in her hand.

"Josh?" she called his name and was answered with only the sound of roosting birds. "Shit." And the others should have been back by now.

THE MASSACRE

BLACKWOOD

He follows the smell of exhaust fumes that hang heavy in the summer air, an almost visible path that shows him the way. He keeps off the road. He's learned the hard way that the best hunters remain hidden. Sometimes the hunter, if seen, can become the hunted.

He carries the sledgehammer like it has always been with him, one hand holding the end of the shaft as it rests on his shoulder. The weight of it makes him feel powerful and adds to the adrenaline surge brought on by the chance to hunt. The rabbit corpses hang from his other shoulder. He hopes he won't need them any longer, but it would be a stupid mistake to dispose of them. Maybe later, if the hunt goes well.

Stalking the stinky one had held no joy for him. The prey had been weak and the kill had lacked any sense of exhilaration. It had been a pointless slaughter and the thought of it actually disgusts him.

As the daylight begins to fade he moves with less caution, the shadows concealing his movements and allowing him to increase his pace. He takes satisfaction in the darkness and the silence it holds. It's as though the other woodland creatures know he is amongst them and have fallen mute in respect of their master. He is the King of the Forest.

He doesn't see the vehicle, but he knows it must be close. He picks up on the odour of engine oil and cooling food. He also picks up on a scent that drives his excitement to higher levels of frenzy.

He can smell cattle.

He moves carefully once again. This is the first hunt in a long time and he has no wish to rush it. He must savour it. He grunts ever so quietly as he approaches for a better view of the prey and the breath catches in his throat.

She is beautiful.

He has found his mate, the one who will rule the village by his side. This one is better than any mother could be. He knows that this one will behave and, if she doesn't, he will soon teach her the need for respect. He also knows that she is with child and this could be a benefit. It is time he had children. It is time he had someone to teach in the ways of the hunt.

She isn't alone.

He watches as she gets in the vehicle and shuts the door. The one who is with her paces up and down as he shakes his head. Then the cattle screams before throwing itself at the closed door.

He moves closer as the dumb animal screams again and starts beating the outside of the vehicle with its fists. Why would it do such a thing? It makes no sense to the hunter.

"HAMMERHEAD!"

The use of his name freezes him to the spot. He hasn't heard cattle speak that word in years and it riles up new emotions of hatred towards the prey. He strokes the hammer shaft in an attempt to calm himself as a seething anger ignites in his gut. He will kill this one and do so slowly.

But not yet.

He will wait for now.

His new mate shouts from inside the van, curse words he has heard many times yet does not understand.

"Wanker." The anger in her voice arouses him and he feels a stirring he hasn't known since many mothers ago.

"Anga," he mimics, the sound distorted and inhuman.

"Anga." He likes the word and repeats it several times as the male cattle stomps away from the vehicle.

He waits, but his new mate remains hidden. He finally decides he must see her up close and leaves his place of secrecy. He is eager to reach out and touch her, but still he moves with the stealth that has served him well in adult life.

As he nears, he can hear her mumbling gently. He reaches the rear of the van and peers inside. She is sleeping and he stares intently at the rise and fall of her breast. Soon she will be his.

As a gift he hangs the dead rabbits at the rear of the vehicle, a sign of his affection for his new mate.

He turns his attention to the scattered bags and the remains of the half eaten meal. He devours the leftovers with gusto, licking the plate clean with the ragged stump of his tongue. With his hunger sated for now, he begins to scavenge. Cattle always bring things he can use in day to day life.

He tips out the contents of a carrier bag, shoving the bag in to his back pocket as he skims over the items. Most of it is useless, but he takes a pocket knife and a lighter. Bored with these, he moves onto the bags, opening them one at a time. He gives the male clothing a quick glance. He can return for this later. The things he wears are getting old and some of this may fit his hulking frame. A thick leather belt does catch his eye and he takes it, putting it around his hips loosely, to save carrying it.

The next bag smells of female and he opens it with keen fingers, pulling out the items that have been touched by his new mate. He finds the soft fabric of lace panties and his breath becomes laboured, holding them to his face and inhaling deeply. He grunts in dismay at the scent of fake flora. He had hoped to bask in her feminine musk. Regardless of this he rams them in his other pocket.

He rises to his full height and gazes in at her one last time before leaving in the direction of the male.

It is time to hunt and kill.

The male has left a trail that a blind badger could follow and he picks up on his scent without a problem. He can never understand why the cattle make themselves smell differently to him. It makes them so easy to find. He doesn't have to go far before he sees his prey and smells the warmth of fresh urine. He is insulted that the cattle dare mark this territory. This place belongs to him, to Hammerhead.

He moves around, hugging close to the trees as he closes in for the strike. The male is facing away from him, its trousers around its ankles as it frantically pulls at its midsection with one hand. He pauses for a while and listens as the male whispers under its breath.

"Katie," it says. "Oh, Katie." This bizarre act confuses him and he almost yells out.

Instead he vents his anger in a positive way, stepping forward as he swings the hammer backwards.

"Katie." As the hammer comes down, the prey moves.

It hits the target, but the blow is only a glancing one to the back of the skull. The cattle staggers as blood runs down its back. He readies himself to take another swing as the cattle takes a forward step. It sways for a moment and then its knees buckle beneath its weight.

He lowers the hammer and studies the body and the strange fluid on its legs and clothing. He has seen blood many times, but it has never looked like this. He bends down and sniffs at the opaque liquid. It smells of nothing. He runs a finger through it and raises it too his mouth, rubbing it on his lips and tasting it.

The cattle moans and he knows he must finish the job. He remembers wanting to make it painful for this one and he has to think fast. He grunts in concentration as he pulls the carrier bag from his back pocket and forces it over the cattle's head. He pulls it tight around the male's neck and drags it towards a young tree, the trunk not much rounder than his arm. He holds the cattle with one hand as it begins to thrash. With his free hand he removes the scavenged belt, wrapping it around the cattle's neck and the trunk. The male begins to fight but he pulls the belt tight and ties it off. The cattle reaches backwards and tries hitting him. He flinches as the fingers tear at his neck, a lucky strike that rips a gash in his already scarred flesh.

He walks around to face his prey, gazing at the panicked face through the transparent plastic.

The cattle raises a hand and tries to tear at the bag in a bid to survive. He can't have that. He retrieves the sledgehammer and lifts it up before bringing it down on one of the cattle's shoulders. The scream is strangled off by the belt, but the sound of shattering bone isn't. He swings the hammer a second time, taking it back and then over in a full roundhouse movement. The head impacts with the other shoulder and rips the arm from its socket, tearing flesh and muscle in a spray of thick red.

He stands over the cattle as the struggling fades to twitching and then nothing. He crouches down and takes another swipe at the white blood. He likes the taste and will have to try and get more.

But first he has work to do and a new mate to collect. The house isn't far and he needs supplies before he can continue. He can leave the cattle here for now.

SIX

"I'm telling you we can save time if we cut through at this point." Curt looked at the map.

"But it's safer to stick to the road," said Judy

"I tell you what." Curt looked at her. "It's getting dark already."

"I can see that."

"So I'll make you a deal." He waited for her to nod before he carried on. "If you still think it's safer walking along the road by the time we get here." He fingered the map. "Well do it your way."

"OK," she replied confidently.

Curt was pleased she was talking again and so far they had discussed everything from music to who was the most boring lecturer at Daventry. He was surprised to find that they agreed on most subjects. They both liked rock music in all its forms and they both had a love for cheesy old TV shows. They had so much in common from favourite foods to pet hates. They couldn't have been better suited and it made him feel good inside.

He'd known her for over a year now and for most of that time he had fancied her, not that he'd ever told her that. In fact he'd never told anyone. For all his tough guy personae, at heart he was just a nice guy who wanted a nice girl. But he had a reputation to keep and he couldn't be seen chasing after girls.

It was OK to be one of the lads and go out on the pull in the hope of getting your leg over, but to be in love at his age was no-no. And so he'd kept it secret, hoping to tell her whilst they were away for the holiday break. Going back to university as a couple would have been acceptable in the eyes of his friends and everything would have been great.

He wanted to tell her now, but with the shadow of the afternoon's events still hanging over them it would be impossible. He knew they'd both been avoiding the subject since the van and he also knew that they couldn't move forward until they faced what he had done. He would have to be the one to bring it up. He just didn't know how to go about it.

He folded the map, tucked it in his waistband and decided to bite the bullet.

"I don't want you to hate me," he blurted and felt like a fucking idiot.

"Why would I hate you?" she asked with a perplexed frown.

"Because of what I did." He paused as he searched for a good way to put it. "Because I killed that guy." There was no good way of admitting manslaughter.

"I don't hate you," she sighed. "It's just that I've never seen someone die." She put her hand in his. "It was the look on his face as it hit the windscreen. I saw his eyes roll up in his head." She shivered.

"I didn't mean to hit him."

"I know that and I don't blame you," said Judy.

"You should blame me," Curt insisted.

In truth he blamed himself, the guilt had been chewing away at his insides ever since. Just another secret he'd keep to himself.

"How can I blame you?" Judy stopped walking and turned to face him. "I didn't make you stop, did I?" Tears filled her eyes. "I could have made you go back, but I let you drive away."

"Jesus, Judy." Curt wanted to pull her close and hold her. "There's no way you can think it was your fault."

"It's as much mine as it is yours," she said and wrapped her arms around his waist.

He stood rigid, unsure of if he should return the gesture. He'd wanted this moment for so long and yet now it was here, in his arms, he had frozen.

Fucking idiot. He scolded himself silently.

"Just hold me," Judy asked softly. "I'll understand if it can't be more, but just hold me."

Curt's heart leapy into his throat at that and he let his arms curl around her shoulders and he held her tightly to him, one hand softly stroking her hair.

"I love you," he said and once again thought 'fucking idiot' to himself.

"I know you do," she whispered back and squeezed him.

"You do?"

"Of course I do," she replied in his ear. "I've seen it in your eyes for the last year."

"Then why didn't you say something?" His voice had taken on an excited school kid tone.

"Because I was worried I'd got it wrong." She pulled away. "I didn't want to look like a fucking idiot."

Curt burst out laughing and Judy punched him playfully in the ribs.

"I hope you're taking the piss," she warned. "It's not a good start for a relationship."

The word relationship filled him with something he could never explain and he didn't need to. Everything was going to be good and he was happy. He laughed harder and he couldn't stop.

"Bastard," Judy nudged him again as she too began to giggle. "Come on, we've got a petrol station to find."

Curt took Judy's hand and, with fingers interlaced, they continued along the country road.

As they walked, the light began to fade from the sky and darkness began to take hold. Curt had handed Judy the empty petrol can, so he could take the torch from his jacket and used it to light the ground in front of them. They had spoken non-stop about family, friends and hopes and dreams. After all this time, Curt was finally getting to know the woman he'd loved for so long and he was loving her even more.

"What about kids?" he asked.

"Shut up," said Judy.

"Only asking," replied Curt apologetically.

"No, listen," she told him. "That's a car." She jumped up and down on the spot.

"We're saved!" cheered Curt.

His feet had started hurting nearly an hour ago, the new trainers rubbing at the back of his heel and his knee was still stiff from the earlier fall. If the car came this way it would save them the rest of the walk and they'd get back to others a damn sight sooner.

"I can see the lights," Judy screamed joyfully.

"Stick your thumb out," Curt suggested, "and show 'em some leg." He began waving the torch above his head.

"Cheeky sod," she laughed as she struck a sexy hitch-hiker pose.

"Work it girl," Curt teased as they both started laughing again.

The car rounded the turn and they were picked out in the glaring high beam as the car slowed down. It pulled up alongside them and the passenger window was rolled down. The man in the driver's seat leaned over his girlfriend and smiled at them.

"Need a lift?" he asked.

"Please," replied Judy.

"Then call a fucking taxi," the man howled at his at own sense of humour and accelerated away, the window sliding smoothly back up on its electric motor.

"CUNT!" Curt yelled after the car, but it disappeared around the next bend.

"What now?" asked Judy as she sat on the damp grass.

"We've got three choices," stated Curt. "We carry on along the road. We cut through the woods and save time or we head back."

"Right now it's up to you," Judy said.

"The woods it is." They left the road.

BLACKWOOD

Shaun Davies was laughing as they pulled away from the two hitchhikers, but the woman in the passenger seat didn't seem impressed with him.

"Do you always have to be such a bastard?" she asked as she fumbled with the packet of cigarettes.

"What?" he chuckled.

"You could have given them a lift."

"Why would I do that, Alison?" he said. "They were probably thieving gypsies."

Alison didn't answer, gripping the filter of one of the menthol smokes and withdrawing it from the box. She cupped a hand around the tip and lit it, drawing in a mouthful of smoke and then blowing it in Shaun's direction.

"How many times have I got to tell you not to smoke in my fucking car?" he snapped at her.

"You can tell me till your blue in the face, but if you want this," she replied, lifted her skirt to reveal that she wasn't wearing panties. "I get to do what I want." She gave him a shit-eating grin.

"It's a filthy habit." He rolled her window back down and coughed.

"So is cheating on your girlfriend," she fired back, satisfied with the frown that creased his brow.

"You're a real bitch sometimes," Shaun said, pushing his foot down on the gas as the approached the next bend.

"Shaun, quit fucking around," Alison shouted at him.

"It's my car, I'll do what I damn well plea..." He didn't get to finish.

The front tires went with a bang, the rubber literally shredding as the steering wheel wrenched itself out of Shaun's grip. Alison screamed as the car swerved off the road, covering her face with her arms. Shaun's mind took long seconds to register what was happening and before he could slam on the brakes they had left the road. The tireless front wheels gouged twin plough marks through the verge and then the world tilted downwards as they entered the ditch.

He stands at the kitchen sink and touches the wound on his neck as he looks at the damage in a section of mirror propped up against an old vase. It's not bad, but he will have to tend to it before the morning. Right now he has far more important things to deal with.

He works by the light given off by the candles he makes himself. They give off a slight perfume of frying cattle fat and it makes him hungry. He ignores the urge to eat. Soon he will feast, but he must work quickly. The new mate won't sleep forever and he must return before she awakes. It will be easier that way.

As he takes the hessian sacks from the cupboard, he hears the sound of grinding metal from the road. He looks up and smiles, the expression creasing the mask that hides his true face. He had forgotten all about the trap he'd laid a few days before on the off chance that cattle would pass through.

More meat for the store, but first the new mate.

"Alison, are you OK?" Shaun asked groggily, his head throbbing from the impact with the steering wheel.

"I can't move my legs, you stupid bastard," she cried.

"Hold on while I get out," he said.

He undid his seat belt and tried the door, relieved to find that it opened with out trouble.

Trouble, he thought, already trying to think of an excuse for having Alison in the car. *Got to cover my own back.*

"Shaun, I can't move my legs." Alison was sobbing.

"Just give me a fucking minute," Shaun growled, the blow to his head hampering the thought process.

He clambered out of the ditch, his feet sliding on the steep, muddy sides. Once out he looked around as he took the mobile phone out of his jacket pocket.

"Shit," he cursed.

"Shaun?" Alison whimpered.

"No signal on my phone," he shouted at her. "Have you got yours?" he turned around on the spot, searching for something. Anything.

"I left it at home," she replied.

"I'll be back in a minute." Through the trees he had seen the faint light coming from a window.

"Don't leave me," begged Alison.

"Listen, I can see a house and they'll have a phone." He tried to keep his tone calm, but he was quickly getting angry at her helpless whinging. "I'll be a few moments."

"What am I supposed to do?"

"Light another fag and shut the fuck up." He walked across the road to the sound of her crying.

He finds everything he needs with ease. It has all been taken from the cattle over the years and he has a hoard of items that eventually come in useful. He puts the thick roll of tape and rope inside one of the bags along with the remaining hessian sacks. He has also chosen a knife. He already has a blade hanging from his belt along with his claw hammer and a screwdriver, so he keeps this one in his free hand.

With the preparations all complete, he blows out all the candles bar one. He sees perfectly well in the dark, but Father always taught him to leave a light on. Sometimes, if you were lucky it would lead unsuspecting cattle right into your lap.

He touches the fresh wound on his neck. It has stopped bleeding, but he'll patch it up when his work for the night is completed. Throwing the sack over one shoulder he turns to the door just as something outside knocks against it.

"Hello." He hears the male voice and approaches the door, laying the sack down on the kitchen table.

"Hello, I need help." He listens as he grasps the door handle, in his

other hand he holds the knife ready to strike.

"Hello." He opens the door and steps forward.

The cattle stares at him with wide eyes, its mouth falling open in surprise. Before the cattle can realise its mistake, he thrusts upwards with the knife, forcing it up through the bottom of the cattle's chin. The blade sinks through the soft flesh and enters the cattle's mouth, slicing the tongue clean in half before it has the chance to scream.

The cattle is strong and kicks out, the foot connecting with his stomach. Pain flares in his midsection and he releases his grip on the knife as he stumbles backwards. He collides with the table and remains there whilst he catches his breath. The cattle had caught him off guard; it won't do so again.

He takes the sledgehammer from its place next to the back door and leaves the house, searching for the cattle. It may be wounded, but it is trying to escape. He can hear it moving back towards the road. He grips the hammer and follows.

Alison tried once again to get her legs free, but they refused to move, pinned just above the knee by the dashboard. She'd stopped crying, her fear replaced by annoyance at Shaun. It was all his fault.

"Let's go to the City," he'd said. "I'll book us a hotel room for the night," he'd promised.

When would she ever learn?

"Where the fuck is he?" she said out loud just so she could hear a voice. Anything was better than the dark silence that enveloped the lopsided car.

She reached up and flicked on the inside light, looking around the interior.

"Where's my bag?" She kept talking to keep her mind off the numbness in her lower legs. "I need a smoke." She searched around, feeling with her fingers for the small leather bag that Shaun had bought her a few weeks ago. "Gotcha." She hooked a finger around the narrow strap and lifted the bag onto her lap.

She lit the cigarette and drew deeply on the minty smoke, holding it in her lungs before exhaling slowly. The window was still open, but she made sure that she blew the smoke towards the driver's side of the car.

"Fuck you, Shaun," she giggled as she sent another stream of smoke into the car.

She heard footsteps up on the road and quickly flicked the cigarette out of the car, waving her hand around to disperse the thick cloud she'd produced.

"SHAUN!" she called, but he didn't reply. "Shaun, don't fuck around," she warned. "This is serious."

She craned her neck to try and see through the rear window, but the interior light gave the appearance of only blackness outside. She could make out movement, but she couldn't make out what it was.

"Shaun?" she whispered as fear crept over her.

She turned the light off again and leaned around in her seat for a better look.

"SHAUN!" she screamed at the sight of his blood-drenched face staring in at her through the back window, his fingers clawing slickly at the glass. She could see the look of terror in his eyes and the knife handle protruding from the bottom of his face.

"SHAUN!" she screamed again, a second before his head exploded across the windscreen, turning it to a spider web of crimson-coated cracks.

He takes great pleasure in watching the head spread its contents; the moonlight highlighting the segments of fractured skull as they float within the dark morass of obliterated brain matter and blood.

He takes an even greater pleasure in hearing the petrified scream of the female within the vehicle. His trap has worked better than he could have ever imagined. It looks like the winter season won't be that bad after all.

He leaves the male to spasm its last and, taking the hammer he jumps into the base of the ditch. He feels the cold wetness of dank water seep through his aged boots, but he doesn't care. His mind is on far more important matters. His mind is on the screaming female.

Alison saw the masked face and the blood stained shirt and her brain threatened to shut down. This couldn't be happening. Not to her. This didn't happen in real life.

Well it is happening, an inner voice screamed, *And you're going to die.*

"Not without a fight." Madness took over as she fished around in the bag. "Not without a fight." She pulled out the small can of deodorant.

"Bastard," she screamed, raising the can in one hand and the lighter in the other.

The flame hits him in the face, but the mask protects him from damage. He feels the heat and he can smell the mask singing at the edges. Then it is gone.

The female has stopped screaming and is looking at him in disbelief.

He leans in and punches her hard on the nose, smashing gristle and bone. She drops her weapon and cups her hands to her face. He takes the can and the lighter and, following by example, he aims it at her.

Alison' head was engulfed in pain, and she could feel blood pouring from her nostrils and over her lips. She sobbed in agony and hoped that nothing else he did could hurt as much as this.

She was wrong.

He jumps up and down as he watches the flames eat away at her face, the hair going up like kindling. She beats at her own head with her hands and her clothing ignites, the flames greedily devouring the fabric and blistering the skin beneath.

Her face transforms as the flesh is consumed, turning black as it burns away from the underlying tissue. She chokes on the mixture of thick smoke that raises from he own body and vomit that slowly cooks in her throat.

He watches as she slumps in the seat yet still she burns, the flames now taking to the seat that holds her dead body. He tires of this quickly and walks away.

He is going to have a busy night.

SEVEN

Katie sat in the van, as she decided on her course of action. She had two choices and neither of them appealed to her very much. She could sit and wait here and hope that somebody returned before the light was totally lost, or she could get off her arse and go and find Josh, who was probably sulking just out of sight.

She didn't like the idea of hanging around. What if Curt and Judy didn't make it back before dark and Josh decided to drag out his newest prank? She'd be sat alone and the thought made her uneasy. She still had images of the crazy man back in the abandoned village and his warnings of the Hammerhead.

That left going out and searching for Josh, which also bothered her. What if the crazy man had been telling the truth? What if the infamous Hammerhead was out there and waiting?

"Don't be stupid," she told herself.

What if Josh is hurt? The thought came from nowhere. *What if he needs your help?*

"OK," she said. "I'll go." She gave into the niggling voice, taking the keys that Curt had left in the ignition and pushing the van door open.

She flicked through the keys until she found the right one and locked up the front on both driver's and passenger's side before moving to the side of the van. She couldn't see what good locking it would do, but she did it anyway. It may have been nothing more than rust on wheels, but there was no point in aggravating Curt. He obviously loved the fucking thing.

The chill was worse outside and she started to wish she'd brought something better than the white, faux-fur body warmer.

She pulled it closed and did the zip up to her neck. It wouldn't stop the slight wind nipping at her arms, but at least her body would be kept warm. She walked around to the back of the van to shut and secure the last door, but as she rounded the end of the van she gasped as she walked directly into something cold and furry.

"Shit!" she yelped, hitting out at the brace of dead rabbits.

As they swung away, she jumped backwards and saw them for what they were, frowning at their presence.

Where had they come from?

She didn't give herself time to answer as she took in the devastation that had been their bags. Clothing and belongings had been scattered everywhere and her anger flared at the sight of her stuff sprawled across the grass.

"JOSH!" she yelled. "You fucking arsehole. This isn't funny."

She may have hit him for the joke he'd played earlier but this was really going to cost him. She quickly set to work on putting all her stuff back into her bag and then guessed at everything else, filling the bags and throwing in the back of the van. Once done, she gave the ground a last once over, hoping she'd not missed anything in the poor light. Only then did she pull the door down and lock it.

The night was rapidly moving in, but the moon above illuminated everything in monotone. She would have liked the torch, but she would have to make do with what she had and just thank her lucky stars that it wasn't a cloudy sky.

Up ahead, she could see the path into the trees that Josh had taken earlier and she headed in the same direction. She wouldn't go too far and she wouldn't waste time on him. If she found him, then he'd get a slap and she'd make him sleep outside. No way was she allowing him back in the van. Not after all the fucking about. He pissed her off at the best of times with his immature attitude and his simpering way of following her around. She knew that he fancied her, but she just didn't see him that way. Hell, she only hung around with him because he was Curt's mate and Judy had the hots for Curt.

You're harsh, girl.

Yeah, well he shouldn't be such a pain in the arse.

Not that Josh was always a pain. He had been the most supportive about her decision to have the baby. She had to give him credit for that. He'd even bought baby clothes and toys for her. In some ways he wasn't that bad. But right now she was angry with him – more than angry. She was furious.

The going got tougher once she ventured into the trees. They were closely spaced and the moonlight struggled to get through the tops. She had to slow down and move carefully. The last thing she needed was a sprained ankle. She used the trunks to hold on to as she stepped over exposed roots and the numerous rabbit holes that cluttered the ground underfoot.

"JOSH!" she called out. "ENOUGH IS ENOUGH!" She waited for a reply but all she heard was the far off hoot of an owl.

"Josh," she said gently, trying a different tack. "If you don't come out I'm going to eat your Snickers bar." She thought about the chocolate and cursed herself for not bringing it along. Then she could have scoffed it down right in front of him.

"Come on, Josh." Nothing but the distant call of the nocturnal bird.

Despite her promise not to go far, she pushed deeper, thankful that the trees began to thin out. The brambles grew thicker at waist level on either side of the narrow path.

Up ahead she could make out the small clearing and she pushed forward. She decided that once there, she'd catch her breath and then she'd make her way back to the van. If Josh insisted on fucking around she wouldn't give him the satisfaction of playing along any longer.

But what if he's hurt somewhere?

If that was the case, she would wait for Curt and Judy to return and then they'd find him together. She'd be no use to an injured Josh on her own anyway. Yes, she'd take a break at the clearing and then forget about him 'til morning. She had to think about herself and the baby inside her. Strolling around the woods in the dark could only end in trouble for all concerned.

With her mind made up, she cleared the brambles and stepped into the small oval shaped area of mossy grass. She saw Josh sat against a tree at the far side.

"Josh?" she said as she walked towards him. "Wake up," she snapped.

And then she noticed the odd angle of his left arm and the ghostly reflection on his strangely shaped head. She stopped and looked at him for a moment as the realisation that something was very wrong slapped her across the face.

"JOSH!" She screamed his name, as she ran the short distance and dropped to her knees at his side.

"JOSH!" She clawed at the bag that covered his head, the plastic slick with congealing blood.

She ripped the bag away and pulled the remnants away to reveal his face; a face that stared back at her with two bulbous, dead eyes. She grabbed him by the shoulders, her hand sinking into the damp wound left by the nearly severed arm.

"WAKE UP!" she screamed as she shook him, refusing to accept that he was dead. "WAKE UP!" she begged, but he would never respond to her voice again.

"WA…" The sentence was cut off by the vicious blow to the base of her neck.

Katie felt a lightning strike of pain with the impact and her vision blurred as fingers of agony raced down her spine and through her skull. She fell forward, her face hitting Josh and she felt his blue lips rub across her own as she slid sideways.

She was hurting, but she held onto consciousness, rolling as she hit the forest floor in an attempt to evade further attack. Who or whatever had killed Josh had obviously returned to the scene of the crime and now he or it wanted to do the same to her. She kept her body moving, losing count of how many times she had turned over and over. Blood pumped in her ears, as she came to a halt and looked up.

"No." The word left her throat as nothing more than a croak when she saw the towering figure drop what he was carrying and move towards her.

In the moonlight his clothes looked stained black, but she had no doubt that he was caked in Josh's blood. It had saturated the tattered shirt he wore and it clung to his well built frame, giving the illusion that he was naked from the waist up.

She tried to scramble backwards on her hands and feet, but the manoeuvre was awkward and he moved faster than she ever could. He swooped down at her and she felt his hand close around her neck, the grip threatening to break her neck. She tried to draw air into her lungs as he lifted her off the ground, standing erect and holding her face level with his.

Katie stared at the emotionless eyes that sat behind the mask of patchwork flesh and she knew she was going to die soon. She thought of her baby and something snapped inside her soul. Primal survival instinct flooded over the more human emotion of fear.

"BASTARD!" she growled and raked at the mask with her fingers, tearing the putrid skin as she forced a thumb forwards.

His grip loosened as she pushed downwards, feeling the eyeball give under the pressure of the manicured nail. Katie heard his guttural howl as her thumb slid easily inside the moist, warm cavity. Then she was falling back to the ground as he flailed at his face in a fit of animalistic fury. Her legs buckled and she fell backwards, landing heavily on a lump and sending a fresh spike of pain up her back.

"Fuck you," she rasped as she sucked in clean air, unsteadily getting to her feet. "Whatever the fuck you are."

The man-thing ceased its howling and turned to face her, half the mask covered in fresh blood that looked like tar.

"Ama ed," It gurgled, the words were only half spoken but the meaning was unmistakable.

"Shit." The truth of the crazy man's words hit her and she ran for the pathway.

Katie had cleared half of the distance and had almost started to believe she would make it, when she was lifted from the floor. She kicked out but hit nothing as she was propelled into the nearest tree. The impact sent her to the brink of unconsciousness, her mind hanging on to the edge of the living world as oblivion threatened to swallow her.

The thing, known as Hammerhead, took her wrist and lifted it above her head. Katie could feel his clammy touch, but the energy to fight had left her. Through half open eyes she saw him take the hammer from his belt and something metallic from his back pocket.

Katie felt the point placed against her palm a moment before he swung the hammer down and her hand was engulfed in fire as the six inch nail tore through, skin, tendon and bone. She screamed herself awake as he struck the nail twice more and then stood back to gaze at her, his head cocked to one side like a puppy that doesn't understand its master's voice.

"Ama ed," he said again as he tapped the hammer against his chest. "Ama ed." With his point made he turned away and went to work on Josh.

Hammerhead emptied the contents of the bag he had dropped next to Josh's body. Using the knife from his belt he cut away the leather belt and dragged the body out straight. With one hand he lifted the upper half of the corpse and struggled to get the first of the other bags over the head and shoulders. He groped around in the dark until he found the roll of tape and bound the bagged section tightly. Once finished he allowed the torso to drop and set about repeating the process on the bottom half.

Katie tried to stand, but any movement caused the pain in her hand to multiply ten fold. She was forced to watch as Josh was wrapped up like some kind of macabre Christmas gift.

She was ready to give up, prepared to let the Hammerhead have his way when she felt the slightest of nudges inside her womb. The baby had kicked her for the first time and the unexpected movement gave her the fuel she needed to do what must be done.

Gritting her teeth against the pain, Katie balled her fist around the nail and pulled. She swallowed the building scream as the steel slid through her flesh and the baby gave her a second, stronger kick. She moaned deep in her throat as the nail head came into contact with the palm of her hand, but she couldn't stop now. Katie took three deep breaths and held the last one. In a swift movement, she ripped her hand free, the nail making a popping sound as it tore out the back of her hand.

As Katie stood she was gripped with a dizzying nausea and she squeezed her fist tight, digging her nails in around the burning wound. Warm blood ran between her fingers and dripped against her leg, but she paid it no notice.

Very slowly, she edged towards the pathway lined with brambles, moving as quietly as she could, keeping a close eye on the Hammerhead as he finished off with Josh. She didn't run until she was at the mouth of the pathway and even then she ran slowly, wanting to get as much distance between herself and the Hammerhead before he realised she was gone. Brambles tore at her bare arms, a minor scratch when compared to the burning hole in her hand.

Katie had made it through the brambles and into the trees before she heard the bellow of frustration behind her. Resting a protective hand on her stomach she ran as if her life depended on it.

It did.

He lifts the meat onto his shoulder and turns around to collect his new mate. For a moment he is confused.

Where is she?

He can see the tree and the nail smeared with her blood, is clearly visible. But she has gone. She will need to be punished, but not in the same way he would punish a mother. This one has shown true strength – she will make a good mate – but she must be shown who is the master. She will have to be broken in before she can take her place in their new kingdom.

He shouts out his anger and, with the meat securely in place, sets out after her. She isn't hard to follow; her fear and her blood leave a mark that is clear to see. He doesn't run. He doesn't need to. There is only one place this path leads and he knows it better than her. He will let her have her chance, give her a sense of freedom before he steals it away from her. It will be her first lesson in who is the boss.

He moves without looking down, every centimetre of the forest ingrained in his memory. He could find her with his eyes closed. He doesn't need to see her because he can hear her breathing. He closes the distance between them without breaking a sweat. Whereas she is weaving wildly from left to right, he takes a direct path between the trees and she doesn't even see him. He keeps pace with her, but remains out of sight.

She is talking in whispers as she runs blindly, but he sees no one else with her. This makes no sense to him, but he doesn't care.

"A female can only be broken if they have hope first," Father had said.

He shifts the weight of the meat from one shoulder to the other without breaking stride. He doesn't want to stop now and let here get away. They are nearing the edge of the forest and soon it will be time for the lesson to begin. He takes the claw hammer from his belt and increases his speed so, as she breaks into open ground, he will be directly behind her.

"Yes," she gasps as she sees the van up ahead.

He steps up next to her and slams the hammer between her shoulder blades. She cries out as she goes stumbling forward, landing with her hands outstretched. He stands above her as she crawls towards what she thinks is safety. He presses a foot down on the centre of her back and flattens her to the ground before moving away and letting her get up again.

"Let them think they can fight you," Father had said.

She makes it three of his paces before he raises his foot again. Once again he squashes her arms out from underneath her body. She grunts in exhaustion and he steps away. This time he lets her get a little further, allowing her to think that she will get away. He raises the booted foot a third time, but she is ready for him and she kicks out at his other leg. The uneven load of the meat assists the force of the blow and he falls backwards, throwing the dead cattle at her as he goes down. The heavy sack hits the target and she is pinned to the ground under the weight of her deceased friend.

He gets up and approaches her as she struggles to escape.

"Then you must hurt them," Father had said.

He crouches next to her and grabs a fist full of hair. He lifts her head back and she screams at him.

"BASTARD."

He smashes her face into the ground, rubbing it from side to side in the hard soil before he lifts it back up. She spits blood and mucus at his masked face. He forces her face into the earth again and this time when he looks at her she only cries.

"Then you must humiliate them and show them they belong to you," Father had said.

He lets go of the matted hair and her head falls loosely to the ground. She looks at his feet as she gasps for air. He stands up and tugs at the zip on his trousers. He pulls out his cock and holds it over her as he urinates on her face and then over her back. He marks his territory well with steaming yellow piss just as Father had taught him all those years ago. Only when he has drained it and shaken it dry does he tuck his manhood back in, leaving the zip open and licking splashes of urine from his fingers.

He doubts that she will be much more trouble, but he has more to do before the sun rises and he can't take the risk of her running away again. He takes the hammer and brings it down on her temple. The blow is gauged well and should only send her limp for hours instead of having to add her to the growing pile of mothers he has accumulated over the years.

Using the lacy panties that smell of flowers he ties her wrists. He drags her upright and throws her over his shoulder. He'll return for the meat and clean up the area later, but for now he kicks the sack of flesh and bones into the underbrush where it will be safe.

As he walks back into the forest, he starts to hum the tune he doesn't quite remember and no one would ever recognize. For the first time in many seasons he is actually feeling happy. He hasn't felt this good since he punished Father that last time. The tune picks up in tempo to match his pace and before he knows it he can see the faint light from the lone candle left burning in the window.

He kicks the door open with his foot and walks into the kitchen, taking the candle and moving through the house. He carries her up the *stairs and along the landing to the only room left with a lockable door. The rest have slowly rotted away over the last few seasons, a decay that matches that of the house and its leaking roof. He will be happy when he takes over the deserted village of Blackwood. The new mate will ensure that the new house is kept clean and tidy, whilst he does what men are meant to do.*

Hunt.

He enters the room and takes her off his shoulder. Any other meat would be left on the floor, but she has shown great resilience and a fighting spirit that has never been matched by any female. He lifts her bound wrists and hangs them over a rusting nail in an exposed ceiling joist. Her feet are left hanging above the floor and he nods to himself, safe in the knowledge that she won't be going anywhere.

He turns to leave and then picks up a scent that makes him reconsider. He walks back towards her, sniffing the air. He grunts and crouches, the sniffing sounds becoming manic as he reaches up under her skirt. He tugs at her underwear, pulling them down her legs and over her ankles with an eagerness that borders on urgency. He remains on his heels as he rubs them over the holes of his flesh mask. This time they smell like he had imagined and he feeds on the aroma as he rubs the moist fabric across his bare lips.

EIGHT

"We should be there by now," Curt said as he studied the map, which they had spread out on the ground. "We must have gone wrong somewhere."

"No shit, Sherlock," Judy grinned despite the stressful feeling that had been slowly riling her over the last half an hour.

"We could head back the way we came," Curt suggested.

"And the main road could be right around the next bend," added Judy.

She had no desire to start traipsing in a backwards direction and probably end up getting even more lost. It was best to press on; the path had to lead somewhere.

"What about Katie and Josh?" As he asked, Curt refolded the map. "They'll be thinking we booked into that hotel for the night."

"In that case we'd better get a move on so we can get back to them." Judy stood up and stretched her back. "They may have had more luck with driver of the car than we did." She couldn't say it without giggling.

"Don't mention him again," Curt said. "If I ever see that car parked up somewhere I'm going to take a shit on the bonnet," he promised seriously and turned Judy's giggle into a full-blown laugh.

"Sometimes, Curt, you're an animal." She slapped his shoulder and he feigned injury.

"And you, my dear lady, are nothing but a spouse beater," he cried out, falling to his knees as he played out the role with the most camp performance he could muster.

"I am not." Judy punched him softly and he fell to the ground whimpering like a hurt puppy.

"No more, please," he begged, holding his hands together as if in prayer.

"Just get up," Judy ordered between laughs. "I don't like leaving Katie alone when she's pregnant."

Curt stopped play acting and got up, picked up the torch and tapped it against his free hand in the hope that the dimming bulb would brighten like they always did in the movies. The trick didn't appear to work in real life and he shone the dull orange light ahead of them.

He looks in the mirror at the ravaged eye socket and the less severe gashes on his neck. Before he goes back out he must carry out repairs to the damage. From beneath the sink, he takes a glass jar and places it on the worktop. He already has the needle and thread ready, but what good are they without patches.

He removes the lid from the jar and, from the clear fluid within, he lifts out a rough square of preserved skin. He lays the flesh patch in the centre of a plate and returns his attention to the mirror. Using a knife, he carefully trims away the strips of hanging skin from around the edges of the wound. He disposes of each strip by placing them in his mouth and chewing slowly as he finishes the job at hand.

Once he is happy with the wound he takes the square of skin and lifts it between two fingers, tilting his head to one side as he spreads it over the top of the wound. He checks it in the mirror, smoothing it out with two fingers before moving on.

He works quickly with the needle, pushing and pulling it through the patch and his own flesh. He has done this many times before and the pain is nothing to him, he works without pause and he never flinches.

When the job is complete he moves his head from side to side, testing the patch for flexibility, ensuring it won't tear away from its new home. It feels stiff against his neck, but like a new pair of shoes, he will soon wear it in.

He takes time to gaze out the window and can see the first hints of the sun returning over the horizon. He has much to do and must do it before the night is over.

He looks into the mirror with his good eye as he pushes a finger into the empty socket, scooping out the remains of the destroyed eyeball. The outer shell of the orb is still attached by tiny red snakes of red and pink. He pulls at it and feels them tug somewhere inside his face. The knife is easier; it cuts through the tendrils with little difficulty and he pops them in his mouth, this time swallowing without chewing.

Using the same needle he pierces through the bottom eyelid and then the top. He repeats the process a dozen or so times as he works from left to right, forcing the eye to close as he pulls each new stitch tight before moving on to the next. He ties it off and admires his handiwork in the mirror.

Now it is time to work.

"What's with Katie anyway?" Curt asked as they walked.

"What do you mean?"

"Well, you're her best friend," Curt added.

"And?" She waited for the next question.

"She must have told you who the father is," he said.

"I know as much as you and it hurts me that she hasn't confided in me," explained Judy. "I mean, she told me she was pregnant before she told you guys, but apart from that nothing."

"Strange."

"Why the sudden interest?" Judy asked him. "Have you got something to hide?"

"No, just curious." He shrugged it off and moved onto favourite films, but it nagged away at the back of his mind.

Curt was one of those people that liked to know things. He didn't do this for the benefit of gossip or hearsay he just liked to know everything. Daventry was a small University and nobody seemed to know anything about Katie and her baby. Whoever had done the deed was also keeping his mouth shut, which was strange since Katie wasn't the quietest girl at the party. She had been known to spread her legs when and if in the right mood and had gained a reputation early on in the year. She had denied the claims, but more than a handful of the lads had confessed to having *'bedded the tramp'*, as they so nicely chose to say it. He'd asked around, but no one was putting their hand up and admitting to it.

"Which way?" Judy stopped walking.

"What?" The question made him realise that he'd hardly heard a word she'd been saying.

"Which way?" she asked again, pointing at the split in the natural path.

"I don't know," Curt replied with a shake of his head. "You chose," he offered.

"Erm." Her brow furrowed as she thought it over.

"Left or right," Curt urged. "Only two choices."

"Left," she said.

"Lead the way, Madam." He bowed and looked up with a smile.

"Fuck that," Judy said. "You're the man and you've got the torch." She stepped aside to allow him to go first.

"I tell you." He tried to hide his hesitation. "We'll go together." He held out his hand and she took it.

"We're off to see the wizard," sang Judy as she swung on Curt's arm. "The wonderful wizard of Oz."

He takes nothing with him. The car is close to the house and he won't have to carry the meat very far. Once more he hums as he leaves the house and hurries towards the road. He wants to finish quickly and return to his new mate. She should awake before day break and he wants to be there for her when she does.

As he draws closer to the road he picks up on the smell of scorched meat and he starts to smack his lips as saliva bubbles at the corners of his mouth. It has been a busy night and he is hungry.

The car is just where he left it and he leaps down into the ditch, reaching in and grabbing the dead female. He tries to drag her from the car but she won't move. Her legs are trapped and he can't free them. He will have to leave her and the thought is upsetting. But at least he can take some of her with him to nibble on as he finishes his work. He uses the knife to slice chunks from her blackened forearms, devouring the first fillet with loud grunts of satisfaction. The rest he tucks inside his shirt for later. Before leaving her he leans over and takes the keys from the ignition, he'll have use for those.

He climbs out of the ditch and gets started with what must be done. He moves the male from the back of the car and lays the body out of the way before returning to the car. He finds the key that fits the boot and opens it, searching for what he hopes will be there. He knows it is there; he can smell its pungent odour.

Reaching in, he takes the plastic container and removes the lid. He splashes the liquid over the inside and the outside of the car. The lighter is still in his pocket and he flicks it to life, holding the flame over the top of the nearly empty container. The fumes ignite with a pop and he tosses the container into the open boot.

He doesn't stay to watch the flames destroy what is left of the car; he still has more to do. He picks the male up by his waistband and carries him back into the woods. As he walks, he takes another section of cooked meat from inside his shirt and feeds.

There is no time wasted disposing of the male in the basement. He chooses to leave the fresh carcass laid out next to the back door. Before leaving, he picks up the sledgehammer from under the kitchen window. Tonight has been full of the unexpected, but if it happens again he will be ready for it.

Father always taught him to learn by his mistakes.

Curt listened to her sing as they started to move uphill. He wasn't sure if that was good or bad. He just silently prayed that they found the main road before the torch batteries died. The moon was better out in the open, but it gave the forest an eerie atmosphere that gave him the creeps.

Judy stopped singing as the gradual slope became a decent incline and she was forced to hum between taking deep breaths. They were both glad when the ground began to level out.

"That's better," said Curt. "My knee couldn't take much more of that."

"It'd better do," Judy looked ahead, "because we're going down again."

Curt could see the path in front of them drop from sight and let out a sigh that said he was pissed off.

"Just give me five minutes," Curt asked and sat down on a length of fallen trunk.

His leg was pounding from his knee to his ankle and he was sure his foot was swelling within the confines of his trainer. He laid the leg out straight and massaged the knee with both hands in an attempt to soothe the pain.

"Curt," Judy said from the top of the slope.

"What?" He made no move to get up.

"You'd better come and see this."

Curt struggled into a standing position and limped over to her side and his spirits lifted.

"Is that what I think it is?" he asked with a grin.

"It may not be the main road, but at least it's a road," Judy confirmed.

"So, what are we wasting time here for?" he took her hand and tugged her on. "Let's go."

Daylight would be with the world very shortly. He hurries as he approaches the area where he'd left the bagged meat and the van. For now he has to push the vehicle out of sight of the road. But he won't have time to destroy it like he had the car. He will, however, have time to scavenge for things he could use from the bags before returning home.

At first he can't remember where he has left the meat and he scours the tree line in a mad panic. He's already had to lose the charred female; he can't accept having to forego another, especially this one. He wants to see if he can get anymore of the white fluid from it. He scrambles around on his hands and knees as he searches the thick tangle of bushes. Then he sees the fox tearing at something and he knows he's found it. He feels anger towards the animal even though he knows that, like him, it has to feed. He creeps up on the fox, lashing out with his foot once he is within striking distance. The animal jumps with a pained yelp as its back snaps like a twig. It lands awkwardly and whimpers, pink froth foaming at its jaws.

He looks down at the fox and he feels something. It may be sorrow, it may be compassion. Whatever the feeling is, he can't allow the beast to suffer. He takes the sledgehammer and brings the shaft down swiftly on its skull. The whimpering ceases and he feels happier again.

The fox has damaged the meat, the bags are torn and sections have been chewed by other vermin in his absence. This is unimportant. Once he has it stored away at home it will be all his. He drags the meat out into the open and takes it back to the van whilst he takes what else he needs.

The anger is flared when he discovers that the van doors are locked. He drops the meat and begins to kick it around in a fit of childish temper. He swings at the rear window with the sledgehammer and sends a shower of ice-like glass into the van. He climbs up and leans in, taking the bags one at a time and throwing them out the window.

He needs clothing for his new mate and he'll take whatever else he can carry.

"I hope it's not far to the main road from here," Curt said, noticing the sky had taken on a lighter tinge since leaving behind the thick coverage of the forest trees, "and when we find a petrol station it better be one with a restaurant next door."

"I just want a nice, hot cup of coffee." Judy kept her pace slow to allow for Curt's knee.

"Yeah, and a full breakfast," he added.

"We'd have to get something for the others," insisted Judy. "We've been gone all night."

"Yeah, whilst they've slept in the back of the van," grumbled Curt. "We've done all the work so we get the full breakfast."

"Okay, grumpy," said Judy. "We'll just make sure we get a muffin each for Katie and Josh."

"If Josh had his way last night Katie will have had her Muffin'," joked Curt.

"See what I mean." Judy stopped and placed her hands on her hips. "You're just vile."

"I know, it's in my genes." He cupped the front of his jeans and grinned.

"What did I ever see in you?" she said, but couldn't hide the smile.

They trudged on and Curt was relieved when the incline began to smooth out near the bottom. They followed the curve of the path and came out near the road.

"Which way?" Judy asked and, in reply, they heard the sound of smashing glass.

They both turned and their hopes were shattered by the sight of the van and the hulking figure leaning in through the rear window.

"What's happening?" gasped Judy.

The figure turned and glared at them from behind the mask of tight flesh.

"I don't know, but he ain't from the AA." Curt took hold of her wrist and urged her to run.

He hears the sound of the female voice and he turns to see the two of them running along the road in the direction of Blackwood. He jumps down from the van with a sigh. At the start of the night, he had wanted nothing more than to hunt, but he is tiring and his patience is wearing thin. With a sigh, he picks up the sledgehammer and heads after them.

He can see that the male is hobbling and he smiles widely. This isn't going to be a hunt. This is going to be a slaughter.

NINE

"What about Katie and Josh?" Judy whined as Curt pulled her along.

"We got to think about us." He glanced over his shoulder and saw the blood drenched figure gaining on them. "This way." He led her off the road and back into the trees.

With his leg the way it was, Curt knew he'd never outrun the hammer-wielding madman. If they had any hope, it was in hiding and attacking first. Judy's question played on his mind as he limped between the trunks with her at his side. If Katie and Josh had been at the van they were surely dead by now. Why else would their pursuer be covered in blood from head to foot?

"We're going to die," Judy screeched and Curt stopped in his tracks, spinning to face her and putting a hand over her mouth.

"You've got to be quiet," he whispered.

In reply she nodded her head, but her eyes had taken on the appearance of an animal caught in the headlights of a speeding car. He could feel her hand shaking in his and he knew she was on the verge of losing it completely. The pointless walking through the night had left them both exhausted, but he had to keep her focused on moving until he found a safe place to rest.

"No more screaming," he told her quietly, removing his hand.

"But it's Hammer…." She began and he slapped her hard across the cheek.

"Just shut the fuck up," he snapped as his own panic overflowed at the sound of heavy footfalls coming from the darkness behind them. "Now move."

He tugged on her arm and she allowed him to lead the way

deeper into the forest as tears streamed down her face. Her mind tried to process what was happening, but the logical part of her brain had shut down to protect her from the truth and she was working on autopilot.

Curt could feel himself slowing down, the pain in his knee reaching a point where it felt as if it would explode at any moment. With each step, the upper half of his leg would be ravaged with a hot poker of agony that ripped up through the muscle and up his back. He knew he would have to stop soon, as he searched frantically for a place to secret themselves from the Hammerhead. He couldn't believe that the shit covered nutter back in Blackwood had been spouting the truth. How could such a thing happen in England? He could believe it of America – the place was fucking huge – but not here. For fuck's sake, they lived on an island! How could someone get away with never being seen? He pushed the thoughts to the back of his mind. He had to concentrate or all was lost.

"There." He pointed and changed direction, limping towards what he hoped would be a temporary salvation.

The tree must have been over a hundred years old and had grown from the side of slight rise in the ground. The roots at its base were exposed in a bird's nest tangle, but Curt hoped they could squeeze in between them.

"Judy," he pushed her forwards and she fought against him.

"No," she hissed at him as she struggled in his arms.

"Do you want to die?" He spat the words in her face.

"No," Judy cried.

"Then get in, now," Curt urged as the sound of the Hammerhead grew louder.

Judy moved slowly and Curt had to push her forwards, but she finally managed to wriggle herself into the damp hollow behind the twisted fingers of the entwined roots.

"Come on," she begged Curt, but he shook his head.

"I won't fit." He'd known this as soon as he saw the hiding place, but he'd had no intention of joining her. "Trust me." He gave her a weak smile as he thought about what he was about to do.

He keeps the distance between them to a minimum; he can't allow himself to indulge in this as a hunt. He hasn't got the time to waste on having fun. He will make it quick and, luckily for the cattle, fast and painless.

For so many seasons now, he has worried that the cattle was becoming less and less. But this single night has been too much. He is getting older now and the new mate's child will have to be taught like Father taught him. It saddens him to think that he won't be the hunter for much longer, but he will take great joy in showing the child how to stalk, kill and butcher.

He pauses, tapping the solid hammer against his shin as he listens for his prey. They have stopped running. Why would they do this? The concept is new to him and he senses that things are not going as he planned. It annoys him that the cattle aren't as predictable as they used to be in Father's time. The hunts are becoming harder as they become rarer. Is this what Father had meant when he'd said that times were changing?

He crouches down and takes a handful of dirt, shifting it between his fingers as he inhales deeply. They have been this way, he hasn't lost them yet. He scans the ground and in the ever increasing morning light he can see their passage through the forest. Scuffed footsteps and broken twigs mark the way like breadcrumbs from lost children. He remains in place as he follows the trail with his eyes and grins behind the mask as he catches the movement of the concealed cattle.

So they want to play a game, do they?

He knows that he should hurry and just make the kill, but the idea of teasing them is too good to ignore. He stands up and walks towards the hiding place they have chosen, turning his head from left to right as if confused. He laughs to himself as he imagines the cattle thinking they have outsmarted him. No cattle is clever enough to do that and they will soon learn the error of their ways.

He reaches the haven they have trapped themselves in and pauses, relishing in the frightened breathing of the female. He grunts, as if in bafflement, and then walks out of their line of sight.

Only then does he bellow like an angry bear, jumping back at them and swinging the hammer at the roots. The female screams as he destroys her sanctuary, her terror fuelling his attack.

Curt climbed the trunk, perched himself on the first substantial branch and waited. He watched the Hammerhead make his way in their direction and pausing to sniff at the ground. Whatever the Hammerhead was under the mask he wasn't all human and the thought filled Curt with dread. This wasn't just a bully that he could beat; this was something else entirely.

As the Hammerhead approached, Curt took a deep breath and held it, looking down and waiting. At first he thought they had done it, the Hammerhead looking around before appearing to leave. Curt let the breath out slowly and then jumped as the Hammerhead screamed out, leaping back and swinging the sledgehammer repeatedly at Judy's hiding place. He heard her scream and he made what could have been the stupidest move of his young life.

He swung his legs and used his arms to throw himself from his perch. His world was stolen by gravity. He fell like a rock and landed on the Hammerhead's back, as the beast prepared to swing the hammer yet again. Before he could be thrown off, Curt wrapped his arms around the Hammerhead's neck and pulled them tight in an attempt to strangle him.

The attack from above is unexpected and he drops the hammer as he tries to reach around and beat at the male hanging from his neck. He feels blindly for anything he can gouge or tear, his fingers sliding into an open mouth. He yanks down on the jaw in the hope of ripping it from the cattle's face. The hold around his neck is quickly weakening him.

Curt tasted the rot on the Hammerhead's fingers as they forced their way into his mouth and worked their way deeper as they pulled downwards. He felt his throat spasm as vomit spewed upwards and he did the only thing he could.

He feels the teeth close down on his fingers and he tries to pull them free, but too late. He howls out in angered pain as the pressure tears through his flesh and tendons before grinding against the bone. The cattle shakes its head viciously from side to side and the fingers are ripped free and blood pumps freely from the wound.

Curt's face was suddenly covered with hot liquid as he spat vomit-covered fingers from his mouth. He refused to let go of the Hammerhead, as the injury sent him into a frenzy of foot stamping. He pulled his arms tighter as the Hammerhead retaliated, ramming Curt's back into the nearest tree trunk. The blow was like a kick in the kidneys and he felt his grip loosen as he fought against a fresh bout of sickness.

He feels the weakness of the cattle and throws it backwards again, his neck finally free as the cattle falls from its place on his back. He turns around and looks down at the bothersome creature. He lashes out with his foot and is overjoyed to feel and hear the breaking of ribs. He kicks again and takes pleasure in the muted grunt of pain that accompanies the blow to the head.

So engrossed is he in the act of retribution that he doesn't see the female crawling from her place of safety.

Judy's mind had left her and she moved with a purpose she never could have believed she had. She scrambled between the shattered root system and, still on her hands and knees, scurried towards the discarded sledgehammer.

She took it in both hands and stood up, feeling the weight of it as she raised it above her head. She took three steps forward and screamed.

"FUCKER." Without waiting for a response she brought the hammer down on the back of its owners head.

For a moment, she was filled with a new panic as the blow seemed to have no effect.

Very slowly, he reaches up and feels at the crack in the back of his head with a three fingered hand. He pushes his fingers between the fractured bone segments of his skull yet feels no pain there. He tries to turn around and face his ambusher, but his vision blurs with the movement.

He teeters from side to side and, as a sigh of surprise leaves his lips, he falls into the void of unconsciousness.

Judy had been forced to almost carry Curt as they headed back towards what they hoped was the road. The left side of his face had already swollen, turning a deep shade of purple and forcing the eye to close as it filled with blood from the ruptured blood vessels.

"Talk to me, Curt," Judy begged.

She knew he was alive, but he hadn't spoken since she'd picked him up off the ground and made him walk.

"That didn't go according to how I planned," he said and spat red coloured phlegm. "Did I get him?" He smiled and flashed a mouthful of bloodied gums and missing teeth.

"Yeah, we got him."

Her assurance was immediately proved a lie as the sound of a pissed off Hammerhead filled the early morning peacefulness.

"Shit," Judy cursed as she attempted to increase the pace.

Curt refused to move and took his arm from around her neck. He pulled the map from his waistband and held it out to her.

"Keep to the roads this time," he said. "Find help."

"No." She shook her head at the thought of leaving him.

"If we stay together he'll get us both," insisted Curt. "You'll move faster on your own."

"No," Judy repeated, but she took the map from him.

She hated what he was suggesting, but she knew he was right. She stepped towards him and hugged him gently, feeling him flinch at the slightest touch.

"I'll come back with help," she promised.

"I'll be waiting," he lied, kissing her on the cheek and pushing her away. "Now, run and don't look back."

With tears blurring her vision she turned away and ran for the road, knowing that she wouldn't stop running until she had reached someone who could help. Far away she could still hear the Hammerhead.

He comes around to find the cattle gone, and a fury builds within him that he can not contain. He gets to his feet and screams out at them, the words are not recognisable, but the hatred behind them is unmistakable.

He bends down and takes the hammer from the ground and swings it above his head as he makes unintelligible threats of pain and suffering.

Curt held his side as he moved away from the road and towards Blackwood, leaving bloodied hand marks as he steadied himself against the numerous trees. He knew he would never see Judy again, but at least he could give her a chance at escape.

He kept his eyes on the ground, shuffling forward slowly but surely, the pain in his knee pushed to one side by the searing fire in his lungs that came with each breath.

At first he didn't notice the change in the ground underfoot, but the morning sun had crept its way into the world. He looked up when he felt its warming rays upon his face.

In the distance, Curt could make out the rooftops of the houses of Blackwood, but he doubted that he'd make it that far out in the open. With that firmly in mind, he made his way from the cover of the forest and stumbled across the hard soil of the field. Once it would have been filled with head high crops, but whatever used to grow there had died and been replaced with waist high weeds.

Curt's breathing began to worsen and he had to keep spitting to clear his nose and throat. He wiped the back of his hand across his tender lips and wasn't surprised to see the smear of bright blood. At least one of his lungs was fucked and the blows to his head had sent him blind in one eye.

To keep moving he set himself a private target and forced himself towards the lonely scarecrow in the centre of the field. If he could make it that far, he would rest for a moment and then set his sights on a new goal.

"Just got to keep going," he whispered to himself.

Three more steps and he fell to his knees at the base of the straw-made man. He cried out as he leaned his head against the post at its feet. He wouldn't be going any further and he knew it.

He knows that the male is injured and won't get far, but still he moves as fast as he can. He can smell the blood they have left behind and he moves after them with a fervent desire to cause pain.

He will let them watch as he eats them as they die. They must be shown that he is superior to them.

The cattle must be punished.

He stops when he reaches the edge of the field and watches the male struggle clumsily away. He can't see the female and is suddenly on alert for another trick. He carefully sniffs at the air and is disturbed that she is not here. She has left her mate alone, which means she could be anywhere.

He will find her, but first he will finish off the male.

He strides across the field, making no attempt to hide his approach. He grunts in anticipation as he nears the cattle and looks down at it in distaste. How could this weak creature fight back so strongly?

The cattle tries to turn around, but it has suffered greatly and the life is quickly draining away from it. He kicks out at the cattle, knocking it over and rolling it on to its back. It must be made to see the end coming.

He lays the hammer to one side and takes the knife from his belt and then sits astride the cattle's legs as it groans wetly. He looks into its face and grins as he plunges the knife into the cattle's gut, working the serrated blade up towards the rib cage.

The cattle coughs up foamy blood, but it doesn't fight anymore. It just looks up at him with glazed eyes as he forces a fist within the wound and draws out a handful of steaming innards.

He brings the fresh offal up to his mouth and bites down on it with relish, savouring the rich taste as the cattle finally expires.

TEN

Katie's hands were numb, but everything from her wrists to her shoulders hurt like hell. The thick ache was the first thing her mind registered as she slowly came back into the world of the living. Her primary reaction was to struggle against the bonds and resulted with the ache flaring into a pins and needle-like fire that rippled through her muscles and tendons.

She groaned as the pain kick started her brain to full alertness and her eyes snapped open to reveal her swaying surrounds. Her thought process was groggy and it took long seconds that felt like an eternity for her to realise that the room was, in fact, stationary. The swaying motion was that of her suspended body.

Katie took a deep breath and told herself to relax, but the exercise had little effect on her shattered nerves. She needed to focus on something, so she attempted to assess her current location. The room was dark; meagre sunlight creeping in through the boards that had been nailed over the window frames. The glass must have been smashed because she could feel a cool breeze stroking her bare arms and legs. The furnishings were old and the smell of damp filled the air, but behind it, Katie picked up on a hint of something foul, a rotten aroma that teased at her nostrils.

She bent her neck backwards and looked up at her outstretched arms and tears threatened when she saw her bloodied wrists tied together with her own underwear, the once white fabric now dirty and stained a brownish red. She let her head fall forwards and watched as her feet swung above the woodworm ridden floorboards.

Katie wept softly as the knowledge that she would probably die where she hung ate away at her sanity, the gentle sobs gradually changing to manic laughter, as all hope was lost. Just as she was about to resign herself to a lonely death in a vermin infested room, something deep inside her stirred and hope became something she was willing to fight for.

She may have been able to accept her own death at the hands of the Hammerhead, but as her baby changed position in her womb she knew she had the responsibility of a life that couldn't fend for itself. If she gave in now, her unborn child would never see the light of day. He or she would never take his or her first breath before screaming out at the world they had just entered. She couldn't and she wouldn't allow that to happen.

Her baby deserved to live and that gave her the strength to do what she did next.

Katie flexed her fingers, slowly at first and then, as she forced the blood to flow into them, increased the rhythm. She wailed as the skin came alive with a thousand pin pricks, but she didn't stop flexing until her fingers once again belonged to her body.

The baby kicked again as if telling her to go for it and Katie responded with a surge of energy that, only moments before, hadn't existed. She stretched upwards with her fingers and felt for the rusted nail that she hung from. Katie used the nail to lift herself up, swinging her weight forward and gradually working the lace bonds nearer to the edge. With each swing her wrists moved only a fraction, but it was still movement. She swung again and the fabric snagged on the head of the nail. Katie craned her neck and saw that freedom was so close yet so far.

"Hold on, baby," she said.

She gripped her hands together around the nail and lifted herself up as far as she could, bending her arms at the elbows to ensure that when she let go all of her weight would be loaded at the point where her wrists were bound.

"Hold on, baby," she whispered and then let go.

Katie fell fast, but not for long. Her arms were jerked above her head and nearly ripped from the sockets as she heard tearing material and then she was falling again. The second fall lasted no longer than the first, her legs hitting the wood and giving out on impact. She fell sideways and rolled onto her back, holding her hands against her stomach and waiting for the baby to tell her it was OK. Katie felt a cold dread, but finally she received a sharp kick from inside and she smiled.

"Good kid," she patted her stomach.

Judy ran along the road and she kept her promise to Curt. She didn't look back. Her legs kept threatening to cramp and her lungs felt as if someone had set them on fire, but still she ran. She gripped the map tightly in her fist like a relay baton. She would never pause to look at it though; she would just keep running until she found the main road. She couldn't afford to stop. If she did that she'd end up like Josh.

Judy shouldn't have stopped at the van, but she did and the image of Josh's head hanging, lopsided from the shroud of hessian bags would never leave her memory. His sightless eyes, bloodshot and dead, his pale face and blue lips would haunt her nightmares and daydreams for as long as she lived.

No, she wouldn't stop running until she found help and maybe then she'd just keep on going until she came to the end of the world and throw herself off the edge and into the abyss.

As Judy ran, the smell of burning grew stronger and the acrid aroma was at its worst as she jogged around the bend in the road and found what was left of the upended car and the smeared stains of dried blood that encircled the wreck. She wasn't planning on stopping, but the nearer she got to the burned out skeleton of metal the slower her pace became, until she found herself walking cautiously around it.

Her foot sent a handful of what she thought was broken glass rolling along the cracked tarmac, but something didn't ring true. Judy bent down and inspected them closely; her gut dry heaved at the discovery that they were teeth, the roots still clinging to miniscule pink mollusc-like pieces of fleshy gum.

Judy stood and backed away from the tiny bones and felt her

rump touch the warm steel of the car's rear end. She jumped and a scream almost left her lungs, but she bit down painfully on her lip to keep it from escaping. She turned around and peered within the confines of the car and saw the twisted form that had once been human. Once again, Judy gagged as her stomach tried to throw up food that wasn't there, acidic bile burning her throat and filling her mouth.

"Oh, God," she rasped, finally recognising the car from the night before.

Would she now be a scorched corpse if the driver had been a more thoughtful sort? Or would her teeth have been pulled from her head and her body never found?

She said a silent prayer for those who had died and asked that she could live to see another day.

Judy was ready to move on when she heard the scream.

He carries both bundles of meat as he heads for home, the bagged up carcass is hanging over his shoulder. The latest kill he holds like a shopping bag, his good hand thrust in through the open stomach wound and the fingers clasping a rib as if it was a handle. The sledgehammer rests between his palm and the still warm flesh of the kill.

He walks steadily along the road for the sake of easiness, no longer bothered about being seen. He can tell the female has passed this way not long ago and he knows that she can't run forever. She'll be his soon enough.

"Fuck it," Katie yelled in frustration upon trying the door to the room and finding it locked. "Fuck it." She took a step away and kicked out next to the handle and the door gave within the frame. "FUCK YOU," she cursed as she kicked again and the aged hinges splintered under the attack, the door falling outwards at an angle.

Katie struggled with the rectangle of timbre until she could squeeze around it and as she stepped out onto the landing she was hit by a stench that had been kept at bay by the breeze in her prison. The rank odour was so strong that even breathing through her mouth offered no respite, the damp atmosphere permeated to the point of being able to taste the sickly flavour of rancid rot and decay.

She didn't want to, but the source of the smell was evident on every spare inch of wall and Katie followed the garlands of withered intestine as it looped its way along the landing. Nails held it in place at regular intervals and, on each hanging section, her captor had attached different trophies from former kills. Some of the body parts were easily recognisable, fresh enough to still resemble what they had looked like in life. Her mind rebelled against the dangling hands, ears and... *Oh my God, was that a penis?*

As her gaze drifted from one atrocity to the next she was thankful when decomposition had eaten away the truth of what she saw.

How long had he been doing this?

How could he have been allowed to do this?

How many people had been slain to fill the walls in such a way?

Katie forced herself to concentrate on getting away from the abattoir scene and told herself to move forward. The floor creaked below her feet, the soggy boards bowing with each step and threatening to collapse under her. She stopped and listened for any sign of the Hammerhead but, apart from her own heartbeat and the sound of constant dripping, the house was silent.

Katie took the remaining distance to the stairs in three long strides and once again waited for a response to her attempted escape, ready for an attack at any moment. When the attack never came, she held a hand to her stomach and took the first step down and moved into a darker level of hell.

The staircase was narrow; a claustrophobic tunnel lined with a hundred eyeless faces that appeared to be screaming for someone to free them from their purgatory.

"Oh, shit," Katie whispered over and over again as she progressed downwards, averting her gaze from the accusing faces of the dead.

The next step cracked below her and tilted. Katie grabbed out for a handrail that had long since been removed as she toppled forwards. Her fingers grasped for anything to cease the momentum of the fall, but only succeeded in stripping the faces away like curling wallpaper.

Katie hung in the air for mere seconds and realised she couldn't stop what was about to happen. All she could do was think about her baby as she screamed out a prolonged *'Noooooooooooo!'*

"KATIE!" Judy knew the sound of her friend's scream and searched the tree line frantically as she tried to locate the direction of the echoing sound.

After seeing Josh's body, she had assumed that Katie had also been murdered. Hearing the scream had given her a glimmer of hope. She had been forced to leave Curt and she was sure that he was dead by now. He'd sacrificed himself so that she could get away. Chance had now offered Judy the opportunity to leave this place with at least one of her friends and she wasn't about to turn her back on it.

"Katie!" called Judy, casting a deeper look at the forest. "Katie!" she called a second time, as she spied the stone structure of the house, camouflaged amongst the trees by a patchy covering of dark green.

The scream had died away and Judy's shouts had received no reply. She stood at the point between road and wilderness, scared to proceed yet just as scared to remain where she was.

"Shit." Judy kicked at the grass and made up here mind. "Ready or not, here I come," she said and ran towards the house in the woods.

The building wasn't that far away from the road, but it sat as if it was part of the surrounding flora and Judy would never have seen it if she hadn't stopped to check out the car and its macabre contents. Now she had it fixed firmly in her sights as she dodged between trees and overgrown bushes. She didn't slow to negotiate the thick brambles, charging through them as they snagged at her coat and jeans.

Judy cleared the trees and entered the uncared-for land that must have been a garden at one point. She was only a hundred yards from the old house when the door began to open.

He hears the sound of his new mate and he knows that she is loose again. He increases his speed, dropping the carved open body so that he can grasp the sledgehammer ready for use. It is clear that he will have to punish her after all.

Katie's scream was cut off as her body impacted with the small landing halfway down the stairs. The old timbre complained and, as she pushed herself upright, it cracked beneath her. She paused, resting her weight on one arm as the cracking was replaced with a complaining creak. Katie sucked in the fetid air from the house and then finally stood. The joists collapsed from under her.

Katie didn't have time to scream before the fall came to an abrupt end, her flailing body landing sideways in the oil-like liquid that swallowed her up with a bubbling splash. The world went dark and her mouth filled with treacle that tasted like death. She fought against the sluggish morass that had enveloped her, screaming out in panic as she tried to determine which way was up.

Katie's feet found the solid bottom and she pushed hard, forcing her head to break the surface. She tried to breathe, but the lumpy fluid filled her airways as she inhaled. Her stomach riled and the mix of beans and spaghetti from the night before exploded upwards, spewing out the foreign mass and saving her life. Without realising it she had grabbed the edge of what appeared to be a sunken pit and she clung to it as she finished vomiting.

Once she could breathe again, she pulled herself free of the dragging contents of the pit and rolled as far as away from it as she could manage. She lay on her back and looked up at the ceiling and the hole she had entered through, watching as dust motes danced in the feeble light above her. She just wanted to close her eyes and make it all go away, but the baby kicked and she cried.

"I'm trying, darling," she tried to convince herself more than the unborn child, "I'm trying."

Katie sat up and wiped the putrid gunk from her face, fighting against the feeling in her gut brought on by the assault of pungent rot that clung to her. She knew what the pit contained; the smell alone was enough to tell her that she was coated in human waste. The basement or what she assumed was the basement wasn't very large, but it was filled with shelves and these were filled with jars.

The owner of the house may have been stark raving mad, but it appeared he was the ordered type. The shelves were all stacked tidily and the jars where grouped in an orderly manner. Most were empty, but the few that held contents were all labelled with dates.

Katie made her way between the shelves, sticking to the middle of the aisle as she passed by rows of bottled eyeballs, fingers and tongues. She noted that none of the dates were current and the most recent was still over three years old.

"Hush little baby don't you cry." Katie began to sing as she made her away towards a set of steps at the other side of the room. "Mummy's gonna sing you a lullaby." She realised she didn't know the words after the opening and started humming the tune, anything to take her mind away from the morbid display of pickled treats.

Katie reached the steps and finally gave into blind panic, throwing caution away as she took the steps two at a time. She barrelled through the door at the top and saw a second door at the opposite side of the kitchen. Katie saw her chance at freedom and, ignoring the gore-laden worktops, went for it.

Judy hesitated, quickly searching for a place to hide as the door swung open.

"JUDY!" screamed a blood soaked Katie as she stepped out

into the sunlight.

"Katie?" Judy stared in disbelief and then ran towards her friend.

She didn't get far before the snare pulled tight around her ankle and the razor-like wire bit into her flesh, cutting through to the bone and threatening to severe her foot. Judy's arms wind milled wildly and she hit the floor face first.

"Katie," Judy called weakly, seeing her friend approaching through blurred vision.

Katie crouched next to the fallen girl she had known since high school and started working at the wire with blood slicked fingers.

"I can't do it," sobbed Katie as she pulled harder.

"PLEASE!" screamed Judy, looking down at the damaged ankle.

"I'm sorry." Katie shook her head as she traced the wire to the spike that had been driven into the ground. "I can't do it." Her hands slid off the spike as she tried to pull it free.

"ARRRGHHH." They both froze at the howl of the Hammerhead.

"I'm sorry," Katie repeated as she stood up.

"Don't leave me," Judy pleaded.

"I'll be back," she promised as she headed back to the house. "I need to cut the wire."

Katie ran back to the house and disappeared inside. She started pulling out drawers in search of anything she could use, but found nothing. She felt around the worktops, her fingers moving through rotten meat that squirmed with unseen maggots.

"The sink," she said out loud, moving up to it and thrusting her hands into the stagnant water that filled it to the brim.

As she felt around, she looked between a gap in the boarded up window and the blood in her veins turned as cold as ice.

He sees the female sat struggling in the garden and laughs at her stupidity, lifting the sledgehammer as he approaches. She doesn't see him coming, too busy trying to free her leg from one of his well-placed snares.

He pauses to watch her and chuckles to himself at her futile efforts. Even a fox would be clever enough to know that the only way to escape is to eat its own leg off. The cattle are a simple breed, they don't know enough to survive in his world.

He swings the hammer upwards and judges the distance between him and the prey. He lowers it once and then brings it back swiftly and, with a mere flick of the wrist, he launches it at the target.

"JUDY, LOOK OUT." He hears the warning and so does the female.

She looks up and the sledgehammer obliterates her face in an eruption of tissue, brain and skull. The body slumps but remains in the sitting position.

As he stomps towards the house, he leans down to regain the hammer and allows himself the joy of fingering the tattered wound left by his well aimed shot.

He stands up and laughs again, licking his fingers as he continues towards the house, throwing the meat onto the pile that is slowing building at the rear of the building.

ELEVEN

Katie's fingers touched upon a handle and she snatched at it, lifting the knife out of the water as her mind tried to think.

She wanted to run and hide, but where could she go within the house? It was his house and he'd find her in the end. She was trapped and the only thing left to do was stand against him.

Not the best idea, screamed an inner voice.

"But it's all I've got," she replied, taking a position that would place her behind the door.

'You going to kick his ass?' asked the voice.

"Maybe," she snapped in a whisper. "Now, shut up."

Katie pressed herself up against the worktop, taking long drawn out breaths through her mouth. Her heart pounded in her chest as the door handle turned with a squeal of protest.

BA BOOM, BA BOOM.

The sound of blood surging through Katie's veins was all she could hear. Her vision blurred and her mind reeled.

BA BOOM, BA BOOM.

The door swung open and the Hammerhead's shadow filled the kitchen floor, the sledgehammer at his side.

BA BOOM, BA BOOM.

The Hammerhead stepped into the room and Katie screamed as she pulled the knife arm back and jumped around to face him. Behind the mask she saw his one eye widen in shock as her arm sped forward. She heard him bellow over the sound of her own heartbeat, as the blade sunk into the side of his neck.

The hammer fell from his grasp as the bellow became a gurgle and he staggered forward, colliding with the kitchen table and spewing blood over the filthy work surface. He turned to face Katie, raising his arms as though to attack. His eye darted around blindly and then rolled upwards to show the bloodshot white.

Katie stood, frozen to the spot as he came for her, his knees buckling before he'd gone two paces. Still he shuffled forward on his knees and then collapsed; his head and shoulders in the doorway.

"Bastard," Katie hissed and kicked him in the side.

She could feel her heart slowing as she realised it was all over and she looked down at the blood and shit encrusted body at her feet. The thought of having to stride over him to get out filled her with disgust, but it had to be done.

'Don't you want to see his real face?' asked the voice.

"Not a fucking chance," she answered and stepped over the corpse.

He lays still and plays possum as the new mate talks to herself. He feels the blow to his side, but doesn't even flinch. He can wait until the right moment to teach her the final lesson. He didn't want it to be this way, but she will have to be punished severely this time. She may even end up in the graveyard of mothers.

He waits until she leaves the ground and is leaping across him, then he strikes. He grabs out and snags an ankle, yanking her backwards with enough strength to dislocate the leg.

She falls on top of him, kicking and thumping as she screams out curses. He loses his grip, pinned underneath her and realising that she has the advantage. Her weight leaves him and he pushes himself up on his hands and knees.

"CUNT," screams the new mate a second before the door is slammed shut, smashing his head between the solid wood and the frame.

"CUNT," she grunts like a beast as she repeatedly beats at his head.

He tries to move, but this is a mistake and the door impacts with the knife handle, sending the blade all the way through and into the timbre frame. He thrashes, as he finds himself pinned like the cattle he has hunted for so long.

"CUNT." Grabbing the handle with one hand, he feels the blow between his legs and howls. His stomach contracts and vomit surges from his mouth.

He slumps, hanging from the blade in his neck.

Katie watched him, waiting for him to move again.

'You going to try that again?" taunted the voice.

"There's got to be another way out of here," she replied, turning to face the hallway and the door at the front of the house. "See, I told you."

Katie limped along the hallway, the pain in her leg flaring to vicious life with each step. She didn't care any more. She had endured so much heartache in her recent life, but she was still alive and so was her baby. That was all that mattered and nothing else.

She paused at the front door and looked over her shoulder at the beast who had taken her friends, slowly crying for them. They had mattered to her, but now they were gone. She was alone and that's how she'd stay.

Katie reached out and turned the door handle, pulling on it only to discover it was sealed shut. She studied the frame and saw the nails that had been hammered in around the edge.

"Shit," she cursed, realising she would have to squeeze past the monster hanging in the rear doorway.

Katie felt the baby kick, the tiniest of movements that proved that the child was still with her. She stroked her stomach and began the journey back along the hallway. The baby kicked again as the figure of the Hammerhead moved. Katie froze and stared in terror as his fingers twitched. She backtracked as his hand moved up to his neck, gripping the knife handle and pulling it free. She gagged, blood spraying from the wound, painting the kitchen wall in a dark, almost black, shade of red.

"No, no, no," she mumbled as she changed direction, running up the stairs before he could turn to face her.

The new mate has hurt him bad and he tastes his own blood as he swallows in an attempt to clear his throat. He drops the knife and moves around the kitchen, throwing open cupboards as he searches for what he needs. He throws the contents of each shelf to the floor in a cascade of shattered glass.

His hand finds the jar and her tears the lid away, throwing it to one side as he scoops the gelatinous, glue-like substance with the hand that now only has two fingers. He smoothes the muck around his neck, ensuring that both entry and exit wounds are well covered. With this done he retrieves the knife and returns to the back door, kneeling beside the meat. He works with proficient ease at the skin, peeling it away from the dead cattle's arm. He takes the strip and shakes it before wrapping it tightly around his neck, pushing it tightly onto the foul smelling glue. The wound burns, but he will live.

The same can't be said for the new mate. She has gone beyond punishment.

Katie took the stairs as fast as she dared, jumping over the hole halfway up and scampering up the remainder on all fours. She was tiring and her breaths were coming deep and ragged as she slowed her pace along the landing.

She could hear the Hammerhead moving around, the sounds of breaking glass and angered howls drifting up through the floor. She considered going back to the room she had awoken in, but the idea made her cringe.

'He's going to get you," sang the inner voice.

"Fuck off."

Katie quickly looked around and chose a room nearest to her. The door was stiff and she had to push against it just to squeeze in. Something snapped under her foot as she climbed through the gap and she felt a cold wetness around her ankle. She dragged the rest of her body inside, ignoring the mess underfoot as she pushed the door shut behind her.

Only then did Katie look down and scream at the sight of her foot wedged on the carved open chest of a young woman. The corpse was old, the skin having turned green and the insides writhed as maggots feasted on the pungent banquet of deceased flesh.

The Hammerhead's footfalls came from the stairs and she backed into the tiny room, a bathroom that had been used as store for human remains. The toilet lid hung to one side, the bowl piled with various sections of decayed remains. The sink was filled with brown water and eyeballs stared up at her as they floated around on the surface.

"Got to hide," she told herself and looked at the bath. "Got to hide."

The top layer of severed limbs had, over time, formed a scab-like crust of brown filth and Katie had to push her fist through it to allow her to get a grip on the bath's contents. She worked as fast as she could, pulling and lifting the varying chunks of putrescent meat to the far end of the bath.

With the upper level removed she had revealed what was below the surface, a pulpy mush of black and green, alive with the movement of every known insect and grub. At that moment, Katie almost backed out, but the sound of the Hammerhead approaching spurred her into action.

"I'm doing this for you baby," she muttered as she swung a leg over the edge of the bath and placed her foot down in the sludge that had once been human innards. "All for you." She brought the other leg up and in, sliding down into the bath and dragging the pile of remains over herself.

As she dragged more limbs over her body Katie wriggled downwards, keeping her legs bent, surrounding her face with a halo of decomposed flesh.

Then all she could do was wait.

He reaches the top of the stairs and looks around with care. He knows she is up here; there is nowhere else for her to go. She has to be in one of the four rooms and there is no escape from him this time.

He walks steadily along the landing and, upon reaching the end, he nudges the door open with the metal head of the hammer. The remains of her underwear lie on the dust covered floor, the only sign that she has ever been in the room. He snorts, picks up the soiled lace and shoves it deep into his pocket before leaving the room.

In the next room, he finds nothing to surprise him. The desiccated remains of Father and Mother are laid in the bed just as he left them many seasons ago and what remains of Simon sits broken in the corner. He sniffs the air like a dog, but the new mate's scent isn't here.

The final bedroom buzzes into life as he kicks open the door and the room is filled with blowflies, irate at the intrusion upon their feeding ground. He casts his gaze around the carpet of flailed skin and leaves his pets to feast.

He turns on his heels and faces the last door. He hasn't used the bathroom for as long as he cares to remember. He always does his mess out in the forest just as Mother Nature intended, and he never feels the need to wash.

He tries the door but it shows no sign of budging when he taps it with his foot. He lashes out violently with the hammer, reducing it to splinters with three well placed swings. What is left hanging in the frame he kicks out of the way as he steps across the threshold.

Where is she?

This one is cleverer than most of the cattle he has tried to tame over the years and, despite his anger, he feels sadness at having to punish her. She would have made an ideal mate and the child would have been strong.

He lays the hammer beside his feet and cups his hands, lowering them into the sink before raising them to his lips. He drinks messily, the algae-tainted water spilling over his masked chin.

Where is she?

She answers his thoughts with a scream of feminine wrath.

Katie laid in the moist squalor and listened to him move from one room to the next, the sound muted as her ears filled with the slime she had immersed herself in. She watched through squinted eyes as he destroyed the door and strode into the bathroom. She held her breath as he drank noisily.

Katie felt her lungs begin to ache through a lack of oxygen and, just as they threatened to explode, she took a deep breath.

Then she screeched like a banshee as she launched herself out of the bath.

The Hammerhead turned and, beneath the mask, his expression was one of shock as Katie swung the naked leg at his face. He reeled backwards as the decomposed foot made contact, the skin below the ankle rupturing and spraying the room with liquefied meat. Katie's scream reached its peak as she swung a second time, the ragged stump leaving her hands as it smashed into the Hammerhead's chin.

The murderer retaliated, attempting to regain his balance, bringing the hammer around. Katie felt the heavy end draw air passed her face, the steel missing her head by millimetres before following its own momentum and imbedding itself in the wall in a shower of ceramic shards.

Katie dodged to the left and let loose with a wild kick into his exposed armpit, hoping to send him further off balance so she could get out of the cramped room. The kick hit the target but the Hammerhead responded quicker than she could have imagined. He released his hold on the hammer shaft and snatched out at her ankle, taking it in both hands.

He growled at her as he threw his weight into her, forcing the leg out at a severe angle as he rammed her into the rear wall. Katie fought back as he tried to wrestle her to the floor, but he was unperturbed by her punching and scratching. He slammed her again into the wall, but she still refused to give in.

Katie reached out for the toilet seat and it came free from the lone hinge. She didn't waste time getting a firm grip of the seat but smashed it sideways against his head.

He released his grip on her leg and charged at her, grabbing her by the throat and lifting her from the floor. He pulled her close enough so that she could feel his hot breath on her face.

Katie looked back at him and waited for the end, as his grip tightened around her neck. She kicked out once and he grunted, pulling her closer as if for a kiss but then threw her away. She hit the boarded up window and the old wood surrendered under the assault.

Sunlight painted her bruised and dirty body as she left house via the bathroom window.

He sees her disappear through the opening and quickly shields his eyes as bright light from above pours into the dark room.

He gazes around the room and rearranges the limbs that have spilled from the bath. In his own way, he likes order and what she has done to his collection is unacceptable. When he is happy that everything is as it should be he approaches the window and leans out over the sill so that he can admire the twisted corpse of what would have been his new mate.

"Arggh," he screams, beating at the window frame at what he sees.

Muttering incoherent obscenities he leaves the room, yanking the sledgehammer from the wall as he storms passed.

For a moment Katie experienced the sensation of being weightless and then it was stolen away by the effects of gravity and the ground came rushing upwards to stop her fall.

She hit the floor and it felt as if every bone in her body had been broken, her skin nothing more than a gossamer bag of bone fragments. Katie took comfort in the knowledge that feeling pain meant she was still alive.

Struggling for breath she rolled onto her front and began to crawl across the ruin of a garden. Every single movement was a torment of agony and she fed on it to keep herself going.

'No pain, no gain,' said the voice in her head.

Katie paid no heed to the voice, focusing instead on the ferns that lined the garden. They offered a temporary sanctuary if she could only reach them before the Hammerhead reached her.

Her body ached from head to toe, but she made herself move faster, the skin on her palms peeling away as she shuffled onwards. Katie heard the monster yell out from the upper floor but she didn't pause to look back.

Almost there.

"Not far now, baby," she wheezed, almost close enough to reach out and touch the vibrant green leaves.

He can't believe that she has survived the fall. He had wanted to take pleasure out of her death, but yet again she has cheated him.

He smashes the hammer against the walls as he moves through the house, wrecking the plaster and leaving a cloud of suffocating dust in his wake. His curses make no sense, a constant tirade of gibberish as the tantrum rages out of control.

He lays waste to the meagre kitchen furniture, splitting the table in two before turning the chairs into kindling. The old porcelain sink goes off like a bomb under the hammer, soaking him with its curdled contents. He doesn't stop until everything has been destroyed. Only then, does he head outside to finish off the new mate.

He'd seen her from the bathroom, a bitch on all fours and that is how she will die. Like an animal. He stomps around to the side of the house, the hammer ready to deliver the killing blow.

"Oooow," he cries out.

He sees the scuff marks on the mossy soil and knows where she has gone. He watches the ferns closely for movement as his hatred and frustration build. He concentrates, listening as he inhales deeply. She is there somewhere and she'll never leave. And, if she is to die, what better place for that to take place than his graveyard.

He tears into the ferns, sinking ankle deep in the swamp-like mush of gore saturated soil. He has used this area to dispose of waste for many seasons, as Father did so before him. He swings the hammer backwards and forwards through the tightly grown underbrush in a desperate hunt for the new mate, pausing every few steps to tear up handfuls of the ferns as a new wave of child-like temper brews in his gut.

He spins around on the spot and stamps his feet up and down at the unfairness of it all, feeling the crunch of aged, brittle bone beneath his soles. He throws the hammer in a fit of rage. He doesn't need it; she will die by his bare hands. He wants to savour the look in her face as the life drains from it.

He begins to move again, crouched over as he fishes amongst the dead for the new mate, wrenching the butchered remains of his victims from the boggy dirt and discarding them over his shoulder.

Katie crawled aimlessly through the festering putrescence, her hands and legs submerged beneath the quagmire of putrid rot. The further she went the worse it became, a heavy stench of noxious gas raising up each time she moved forward. Nothing here resembled human remains, the flesh of the dead having dissolved into nothing more than a rank liquid of maggot infested shit.

She cried softly, the tears streaking her gore covered face with tiny roadways of dirty pink. She knew it was useless yet she forced herself to keep moving, her entire frame racked with pain. Beneath her gentle sobs Katie hummed the lullaby she couldn't remember the words too, repeating the same line over and over again in her mind. Anything to shut out the images of her impending death.

She could hear the Hammerhead ranting, the gargled threats growing louder as he closed in on her. With a final effort of pure will she lay down and dragged her body into the tangle of brambles, the thorny branches nipping at her bare arms and legs as she tried to hide from the monster. She felt warmness between her legs and cried at the thought of having pissed herself, a final humiliation before her life is finished.

He can smell her fear and something stronger, something that tweaks at his nostrils and replaces his anger with excitement. The aroma is so clear that he doesn't have to search for her anymore. He stands upright and trudges towards where she is, a smile on his scabrous lips.

As he draws near he can hear her quietly crying a tune, one he has sang himself many times yet never in such a sweet way. He can't remember where he first heard it, but he associates the sound with pain and torture.

He looms above the waist high thicket of brambles and he can see he curled up body in the shadows below. He bellows out in triumph, thrusting and arm downwards and grabbing her arm. She screams weakly as he jerks her upwards, shaking her violently to ensure maximum damage as he drags her through the vicious barbs of entwined branches.

Katie saw him and tried not to move, but it was too late. The Hammerhead had seen her and he lunged towards her. She screamed as she was torn upwards, something in her shoulder popping painfully as he snatched her from the ground.

As she cleared the brambles he tossed her to one side and she hit the moist ground face first, her nostrils filling with slime as she attempted to breathe. Before Katie could roll over she felt his weight on her back and his fist pulling at her hair.

He worked something around her neck with his free hand and then released his grip on her hair. As her head fell back into the deathly slime she gasped. He tightened the thick bramble like a noose and a hundred pins tore into her tender skin.

Katie thrashed below him, but he leaned down hard in the small of her back and drew the spiked garrotte even tighter. She closed her eyes and said a prayer as things began to fade away.

He feels her struggles weaken and grins with pleasure as she goes limp, her arms falling motionless as he gives a final tug on the bramble around her neck.

He leans forwards and licks the stump of his tongue along the base of her neck. In his state of rising excitement, he doesn't see the slight twitch in her hand as it clenches around the dagger like section of bone.

Katie was on the verge of oblivion when the stranglehold was removed. She lay motionless as the Hammerhead nuzzled at her shoulders and neck, his saliva trickling over her filthy skin in thick rivulets. She felt the sudden hardness between his legs digging into her buttocks and something snapped inside, her humanity suddenly replaced by something primal and dangerous. In that instant, she became like him.

The Hammerhead began moving up and down, heavy grunts whispered in her ear as he masturbated against her. She held the fresh scream in her throat as she gripped the section of bone in her hand and rammed it upwards at his face.

His weight fell away from her and she kicked out at him,

turning to see him kneeling at her side as he pulled at the bone that protruded from his good eye. She lashed out again with her foot, hitting the bone and pushing it deeper into the ruined socket.

Katie scuttled away from him as he stopped thrashing, his arms falling to his side and his head cocking to the left. She moved as quickly as she could and he smiled, turning to face her.

He may be blind but he can hear her and he can smell her. He is a hunter of many senses and she won't escape that easily.

Katie got to her feet unsteadily and turned to run, but the Hammerhead tracked her every movement. Running was impossible, her feet sinking into the morass of decay and slowing her down.

The Hammerhead was on her before she could clear the ferns, wrapping his arms around her stomach and lifting her upward, in a violent bear hug. The grip forced the air from her lungs and she lost the ability to inhale as he squashed her in his vice-like arms.

"Don't hurt my baby," Katie gasped as she reached behind and found the end of the bone knife.

She slammed her palm against the end and, for a second, his grip loosened as he howled in her ear, leaning his head forward and sinking his teeth into her lacerated neck. She found the edge of the mask and stuffed her fingers between the stitching and pulled as hard as she could.

"Don't hurt my baby."

He feels the stitches tear through his flesh as she pulls away the many layers of patchwork mask he has applied over the seasons. He drops her, trying to replace the skin, but the mask falls away to reveal a visage of pus filled scars and gangrenous boils.

The exposed rot of his face flares in white hot agony and he snatches out blindly at the female.

"DON'T HURT MY BABY!" Katie screamed as she regained her breath, seeing the discarded sledgehammer and limping towards it.

The blinded Hammerhead came after her, the tattered mask hanging from his chin and flapping against his chest.

"Not my baby." Katie picked up the hammer and hefted it above her head, turning as the Hammerhead came charging forward.

"NOT MY BABY!" The sledgehammer came down on his shoulder and Katie yelped as she heard the satisfying sound of shattering bone.

"NOT MY BABY!" She raised the weapon again and brought it down on his chest, the ribs caving in as the Hammerhead fell to his knees with a wheezing breath, thick red blood spraying from between his lips.

"NOT MY BABY!" The sentence became a prayer as she swung again, smashing open his skull. "NOT MY BABY." She didn't stop until his body was broken and submerged in his own graveyard.

He falls backwards as the blows rain down on him.

The hunt is finally over.

Katie limped away from the house and back to the road. He was dead this time; she'd made sure of that. She still held the sledgehammer in her right hand, dragging the end along the floor, but refusing to let go.

"All for you, baby," she whispered, resting the other hand on the top of her distended stomach. "All for you."

EPILOGUE

DAVENTRY UNIVERSITY

It had been six months since the events in Blackwood and Katie had finally decided it was time to return. She had been scarred in more ways than one but she had to face the future.

Katie had parked the car near the main entrance and now she walked along the hallway, pushing the pram as she ignored the stares of pupils and lecturers alike. The place hasn't changed at all in her absence, but it feels different to her, almost unreal in its normalcy. She has seen things these people couldn't ever imagine in their darkest nightmares and it has changed her. She is stronger now than she's ever been and that is why she has returned.

She follows the corridor she knows so well yet hardly recognises, her gaze fixed on the glass-panelled door at the end. As she approaches she reads the black lettering across the frosted pane.

Professor D Reilly

She raps on the glass and enters without waiting for an invite, pushing the door open with her rump and pulling the pram in with her.

"Katie," he states, clearly surprised to see her. "How are you doing?" he stammers. "How are you coping?"

"Getting by," she replies in an attempt at small talk. "It's weird what seeing all your friends die does to you," she adds sarcastically.

The professor takes a handkerchief from his jacket pocket and mops at the sweat on his brow. Katie is the last person he expected to walk into his office and, not only does he dread to think what she wants, but he isn't about to waste time finding out.

"If it's money you want," he says, "I'm more than willing to help you with the baby."

"I don't want anything from you," she sneers as she leans over the pram. "I just wanted you to see our son." She lifts the blanket wrapped child and cuddles him closely to her bosom.

"But I want to help."

"I called him Edward," she says, ignoring his insincere words.

Katie holds the child out and Reilly stands, taking him from her before returning to his seat. He pulls back the blue woollen blanket.

"What the…" Reilly gags.

"He was stillborn," Katie explains.

Reilly looks up questioningly and his eyes widened as the sledgehammer sails towards his head.

Katie returns to the car and secures Edward in the passenger seat. She folds down the pram and puts it the boot. She climbs in the driver's side and smiles at her son as she starts the car.

"Hush little baby, don't you cry. Mummy's gonna sing you a lullaby." She forgets the rest and hums the tune as she pulls into traffic.

It's time to go home.

THE ULTIMATE UK HORROR MAGAZINE
GOREZONE
GZ

GZ
THE ULTIMATE UK HORROR MAGAZINE
www.gorezone.co.uk